Hoofbeats

Katie and the Mustang

Book Four

by KATHLEEN DUEY

DUTTON CHILDREN'S BOOKS
NEW YORK

CIP Data is available.

Published simultaneously by Dutton Children's Books and Puffin Books, divisions of Penguin Young Readers Group
345 Hudson Street, New York, New York 10014
www.penguin.com

Printed in USA · First Edition

10 9 8 7 6 5 4 3 2 1

ISBN 0-525-47275-4

My childhood memories are set to hoofbeats:
a fog-softened gallop on a lonely morning; the joyous
clatter of friends pounding down the Canal Road;
a measured, hollow clop of a miles-to-go July afternoon;
the snow-muffled hoofbeats of wintertime; the squelching
rhythm of a close race with a rainstorm. These books
are for my dear friends, the horses of my childhood—
Buck, Ginger, Steve, and Cherokee Star.

Thank you all.

CHAPTER ONE

🐉 🐉 🐉

The little one walks beside me every day. Her soft feet make almost no sound in the dust. We have passed through good grass into badlands. The scent of sage is stronger every day. When will we see the mountains?

*W*e stayed at Fort Laramie three days. The McMahons were fussing with a sore-hoofed ox, Andrew Kyler had a broken water barrel, wheel rims were loose—the troubles went on and on.

Mrs. Kyler and I spent two days washing every single-bingle piece of clothing in the wagon, cleaning the dirt and bugs out of the jockey box, sharpening knives, rearranging the tangled mess of her belongings, beating the dust from the feather bed, her blankets, and the quilts. I washed my blanket in the Laramie River, leaning out over the water with Mrs. Kyler holding my ankles so I wouldn't fall in. We did all the things we hadn't had time or strength to do while we were traveling. I reread two stories from my mother's book in the evenings.

Mrs. Kyler had hoped to buy a few things at the post store, but the prices were too steep—ten to twenty times more than the cost of the same goods back in the other towns we'd passed through. She had hoped to sell a few of her extra things, as well, but the post trader wasn't buying anything from anyone. People with overloaded wagons had only had one option left. Weight was killing the oxen.

I heard the Craggetts arguing over leaving behind a caned rocking chair that had belonged to her grandmother. Their oxen were wearing thin already—Mrs. Craggett had packed all her household treasures. I wondered about Mrs. Stevens. There was no way to know if she and Mr. Stevens were behind us on the trail or ahead of us—or if they had decided to turn back long ago. Had they found a big party to travel with? Had Mrs. Stevens tried to bring all her things?

The guide we thought about joining turned out to be a man of hard opinions, determined to take a wagon cutoff he'd heard about from a friend of a friend of his. He said it was brand-spankin' new, just discovered, and that it'd cut a hundred miles off the journey.

Not even Mr. Silas thought that was a grand idea, chasing down some route the guide himself didn't know. So Mr. Kyler thanked him and sent him back to the party he was leading.

New wagon parties arrived once or twice a day while we were at Fort Laramie. Most were Mormon folks. Some barely stopped. Others circled their wagons and camped as we had. When I walked the Mustang out to graze, I saw people standing beside their wagons in the mornings, stretching and talking, enjoying a morning without the constant hurry to keep moving.

On the afternoon we left, we could see wagons lined up before us on the trail, like beads on a necklace. Looking back brought the same view. The menfolk stopped arguing about getting a guide. From here on, at least until Fort Bridger, there would be help in sight in any direction and no doubt at all about where the best route lay.

"There are only fourteen of us," Mrs. Kyler said to me that afternoon. She was walking behind the wagon as she did sometimes to stretch and get away from the endless jolting of the wooden wheels.

I looked up at her and nodded. She ticked the names off on her fingers. "Six wagons full of us Kylers, then one for Mr. Silas and his partners, one each for the Craggetts, the Heldons..."

And as she went on down the list, I thought about the odd combination of people who had decided to go on together. Starting at the front of the wagon line, there were six Kyler wagons with me walking somewhere alongside, ranging wide to find grass for the Mustang whenever I could. Andrew came behind, usually, herding his stock. Julia, Polly, Hope, and the younger Kyler girls usually walked together behind one of the Kylers' wagons.

Then there was Mr. Silas and his three partners, bearded, rough-spoken, and private. They pretty much kept to their own campfire at night, talking in low voices about business and cattle and the war in Mexico and who knew what all else. I listened to them when I could, but if they noticed me grazing the Mustang nearby, they'd wave me off.

There were our mileage keepers—the Taylor family—with their four children, their pale daughter

Mary riding inside the wagon, often lying down, the rest walking. I felt so sorry for Mary. She smiled at me when she saw me, gentle as spring rain. I always smiled and waved back, but I never really talked to her much. I wish I had.

The McMahons were next—big, comfortable folks with a funny and adorable little son named Toby. I loved the way they talked about everything, the way Mr. McMahon always let his wife speak her mind. Then came the Craggetts. Mrs. Craggett was so proper that I knew she would hate Liddy McKenna forever for being different from most women she knew, no matter how many times Liddy and her big draft mare pulled a wagon out of deep sand or offered some other neighborly help.

Then came the Heldons—Grover and his parents. I hated Mr. Heldon for the bruises on Grover's face. And I was afraid of Grover, because he was the meanest boy I had ever known. I wished, more than once, that they would find another wagon party to travel with, but they stayed with us.

Miss Liddy McKenna's three wagons came last. She drove one, a Negro man drove the second, and an odd-looking man with big hands and feet drove the last one. There was a third man with blond hair pulled back in rawhide tie like a trapper. I had noticed the Negro man limping at Fort Laramie. I didn't know how he had gotten hurt, and I hadn't heard anyone else talking about it, either.

People acted like the circus folks weren't there, bringing up the rear, camping separately—unless help was needed. Except for Miss Liddy McKenna, I didn't know their names. I wasn't sure anyone did. They'd been around fever deaths before they'd joined us, and no one wanted to associate with them, but no one had objected too much. It was a comfort to have three more wagons, even if they weren't proper, covered wagons and carried loads of circus-show costumes and cracked corn for their fancy horses instead of farm tools and quilts.

Mrs. Kyler had fallen silent when I looked up from my thoughts. She was watching me.

I smiled. "I was just thinking about everyone." I made a wide gesture with one hand.

"It's an interesting batch, all right." She smiled. "I admire that Miss Liddy, but don't tell my husband that." She lowered her voice. "Women can do lots more than most men like to admit."

"I keep hoping they'll decide to give us their show," Mrs. Kyler said.

I smiled at her. "I would love that!"

She nodded. "We all would, I think. I wondered why they didn't offer to back at the fort. There would have been quite a crowd. Maybe because Mr. Le Croix twisted his ankle."

"Mr. Le Croix?" I echoed.

"Mr. Pierre Le Croix. He said it rhymes with 'the boy.' Le Croix! He came here from France," Mrs. Kyler said. "I didn't know there were Negroes in France." She smiled. "Of course I can't think of anything I do know about France except that they gave old Ben Franklin enough money for troops and food so we could win our revolution."

I stared at her. "Mr. Le Croix," I said, as much to myself as to Mrs. Kyler. "Do you know the other two men's names?"

She nodded. "Miss Liddy got to talking to Andrew about horses one day at the fort. I was close by, so I asked. The blond-haired man is Mr. Jacob Swann, and the tall man is James Dillard."

I sighed. Miss Liddy and I had only spoken the one time, when she asked about the Mustang, and had said she was an orphan, too. I wanted to talk to her. But truth was, it scared me to be around her, to be around any of them. Fever terrified me. I couldn't think about it without remembering my family, how fast they had gotten terribly sick, how quickly they had been gone.

"Are you all right?" Mrs. Kyler asked me again.

I nodded.

"Thinking about your family?"

I glanced up. I had never talked to anyone about losing my family except Hiram a little—and the Mustang. I couldn't see that it would do any good to share my troubles with Mrs. Kyler. She had enough of her own. So I shook my head. She reached out and patted my arm.

All that first week out of Fort Laramie, we had parties of Mormon folks close behind and before us. I saw the men pushing the harness bars of their odd little horseless carts day after day. I was amazed to imagine their weariness and suffering; watching them ford the Platte River worried me, but all made it safely, as did we. There was a makeshift ferry but the water was low and we didn't use it.

We headed southwest to find the Sweetwater

River, then followed it, keeping enough distance between the parties to let the dust settle a little. It was terrible. Sometimes it was so thick Mrs. Kyler would loan me a linen kerchief to tie over my mouth and nose. We'd wet the cloth. It helped, but our eyes itched and watered constantly from the grit. The wagon canvas turned brown with it; it rimmed the Mustang's nostrils.

He and I had it better than most. I could walk away from the wagons to where the dust thinned out a little. I pitied the wagon drivers. And I pitied poor Mary Taylor most of all. I could hear her coughing at night.

The Sweetwater River had clean, clear water that was cold in the mornings and still cool in the hot afternoons. With the good water, there was better grass. I kept the Mustang grazing every second of the day that I could. He was thinner, but seemed fresh and ready to travel every day at dawn, calling to the mares when I led him away from our little half circle of wagons. We didn't have enough to make a full circle anymore.

"You keep an eye out for snakes," Mr. Kyler warned me one morning.

I looked at him. "Rattlesnakes?" I asked. There had been some in parts of Iowa, I knew. But I had never seen one.

"The rattlers get thicker as we go, a man at Fort Laramie told me. They like the sage and the rock."

I swallowed hard and nodded. Snakes. Why hadn't I thought about it myself?

"A big enough rattler can lame a horse so's he needs to be shot. It'd kill you. I wish Hiram and Annie could have come," he added, as though thinking about snakes somehow led to it. I knew what he meant, though. He liked me, but I was one more child to worry about, and he had no time to look after his own granddaughters the way he wanted to. If Hiram and Annie had come, Hiram would have been responsible for me.

"I'll be all right," I said evenly.

He smiled wearily, then Mr. Silas shouted his name and he turned to go see what was wrong.

Sixty long, sun-stricken miles along the Sweetwater River, traveling through brittle grass and leathery sage, brought us to Independence Rock, a shapeless mound of brownish stone. The boys and men swarmed over it like ants on spilled sugar, looking for places to carve their names.

I led the Mustang closer, reading the letters gouged into the rock with knives and chisels and pry bars. There were messages that made my heart ache. *"Margaret died,"* one said. *"I am going home."*

Others were almost funny. *"Oregon, by gum"* some-one had written. The first *"O"* was four times as big as the other letters. I wondered if the person who inscribed it had started off with big intentions, then realized how hard the rock really was and made the rest of the letters smaller.

I could hear voices coming from all over the rock, people were reading inscriptions aloud, calling out names and places, reading messages left for rela-tives and friends.

After Independence Rock we came to a pair of stone gates—or so it looked to my fanciful mind. The Sweetwater had worn a narrow opening in high cliffs of stone. People called it Devil's Gate. We couldn't go through it; there was no bank along the river-side to follow. We went around it instead, and soon saw the tracks of those who had come before us, mark-ing the way. The ground was rough and sloped.

Coming back up the hill on the far side, one of

Andrew's herd mares slid sideward and fell, squealing in pain. She struggled back upright, then stood, trembling, holding one back leg at an odd angle, her hoof not touching the ground.

When a horse ruins a leg, it is impossible to save its life. It cannot heal, and it will only be in terrible pain as it starves to death, unable to walk and graze. I know that is a terrible thing to say, but it is true, even on a farm when there was not the pressing need to keep moving that we had.

I remembered my father shooting a horse because it had broken its leg, and as much as it upset him, that's what Andrew Kyler had to do.

I led the Mustang away when I saw Andrew walking back to his wagon for his gun, running as fast as I could over the rocky ground. By the time we heard the shot, it was dimmed by distance. I still flinched. I saw Andrew later that day, and his eyes were deep and sad. The mare had been a favorite of his, a sweet-natured animal.

After the Devil's Gate was behind us, we passed onto a sage desert so dry that my lips dried, then cracked. I had a fissure in my lower lip that broke open and bled a little most mornings when I yawned.

The earth beneath the oxen's hooves turned to sand as we traveled. There were rocky ridges, steep-sided ravines and bluffs as far as the eye could go—and beyond that, almost at the horizon, were bluish mountains peaks jutting skyward. We all stared. None of us had ever seen mountains.

It just seemed impossible to me. How could dirt and rock get piled up like that? I was amazed at how the peaks got a little bigger with each day's progress, too. One day we could see clearly that the tops were white.

Miss Liddy noticed my staring at them one day during dinner break. I had eaten, and I was leading the Mustang past her camp to go look for grass.

"It's snow," she called to me.

"Not in the middle of July," I corrected her. I stopped a good ways back, uneasy being so close to her camp.

She smiled and nodded without coming nearer. I was grateful. "What else could it be, Katie?"

I shrugged. "White rock? Or salt? Like the lake where the Mormon people are building their city?"

She grinned. "Want to bet?"

I shook my head, flushing. "Betting wasn't allowed

in my family. No kind of gambling was."

Miss Liddy laughed aloud. "But you're taking a big risk coming west. That's a gamble—you're betting that everything will come out all right."

I shrugged, knowing my parents would scold me for even talking about gambling. It seemed to me that Miss Liddy was right in a way, though. Anyone who came west was willing to take chances or they would have stayed home.

"They all say the worst part is the last," Miss Liddy said quietly.

I had heard the same thing. The Mustang was holding up, healthy and sound. But looking around at the heat shimmers already rising off the dry soil, I wondered if we would all make it to Oregon. Some days I was so weary and discouraged that I wondered if any of us would.

CHAPTER TWO

❧ ❧ ❧

*The land is dust dry, and the scent of sage covers
all others. Sometimes on the wind I can smell
pine trees. I try to travel faster, but the little one
holds me to the pace of the oxen.*

"Never saw a stallion as tame as that one is,"
Mr. Taylor called to me one morning as we
broke camp.

I looked at him. "He's not all that tame. He just
trusts me, I guess."

Mr. Taylor shrugged. "You ought to let one of the
men break him so you could ride. He wouldn't be
much burdened, a little thing like you."

"I don't mind walking," I said, and I meant it. I
was so used to walking that when I did have to ride

in the wagon for a stretch, the jouncing made my stomach sick. I told him that.

"You'd like riding a horse better than being in the wagons," he said, laughing.

I smiled at him so that he wouldn't think I was rude, but I wanted to walk away because I had just noticed Grover on the far side of the wagon, walking with his head down. Was he listening? I watched him for a few seconds; he wasn't looking in my direction as he went back to his chores.

"Would you look at that," Mr. Taylor said, smiling, and he waved one hand at Miss Liddy's wagons, then walked off to help his wife finish reloading their wagon.

I followed the direction of his gesture and saw Miss Liddy McKenna, mounted on the huge mare, riding astride in her trousers, without bit, bridle, or saddle. I stared. I had seen her ride the big mare this way many times now—everyone had. It never lost its charm for me, to see the horse cooperating out of respect and love like that, not fear of leather whips or metal bits. I sighed. Riding a horse like that, with trust and respect...

I touched the Mustang's cheek, and he turned

toward me as he usually did, to nuzzle my shoulder. "Would you *let* me ride you?" I asked him, then blushed when I heard Grover laugh out loud.

"Nooo, I doooon't want you to ride meeee," he answered, making his voice into a quavering whinny sound. His face was twisted into a taunting grimace.

I led the Mustang away without a word to him. I was furious with myself. The truth was that I *did* talk to the Mustang like he was a person. I was so much in the habit of it that I didn't even realize I was doing it.

"I have to be more careful," I said to the Mustang, then I blushed and glanced around.

Polly and Julia were together as usual, standing near Polly's parents' wagon, sorting through a basket of berries they had picked along the river the day before. Polly's tiny mother was sitting on a log, mending, her needle flashing in the early sun.

No one was looking toward me. They rarely did. Nothing had changed. They weren't ever mean to me. It was more like I was invisible to the Kyler girls. I slid my hand beneath the Mustang's mane and felt the warmth of his coat against the palm of my hand.

I had thought about it a lot. I knew part of the

reason none of them had bothered to become my friend was that they had one another. They had all known one another all their lives, and they were as close as peas in a pod.

Another reason was that I was rarely without the Mustang at my side. I had to take care of him—not play silly games. From the time I'd met them, I'd had to spend most of every day finding grass for the Mustang. I couldn't race between the wagons or have contests to see who could find the most firewood or buffalo chips. I couldn't play hide-and-seek on our dinner stops, either. I was busy helping their grandmother make supper, then clean up. Their mothers let them go play together before bedtime. That was when I was helping Mrs. Kyler ready the wagon for morning, repacking the jockey box and getting the stallion settled with the mares and Andrew's horses for the night.

The Kyler girls were playing and giggling less than they had at the beginning of the journey, though. They were tired in the evenings, wrung out by the heat of the day. We all were. The searing hot sun was affecting everyone's spirits.

As the days dragged past and the weather got

hotter and hotter, sometimes you couldn't hear anyone talking at all in our evening camps. Some nights, people just ate, then stared into the flames for five or ten minutes and went along to bed without saying a word to anyone.

Once in a while, Mrs. Kyler would notice that her granddaughters were ignoring me, and she would repeat her offer to speak to them on my behalf. I always begged her not to. I wasn't sure I wanted them for friends at all—but even if I did, having her say something to them would hardly help. If anything, it would make them dislike me.

I envied all the Kyler girls. None of them had lost their parents and a sister like I had. None of them had ever had to live with cruel strangers. The closest misfortune had come to any of them had been Annie's accident. And as awful as that had been, Annie was probably on the mend, and she had Hiram's love to see her through. As always, when I thought of Hiram and Annie, I hoped that they were both well and that Annie's burns were completely healed.

"I hope I can see them again someday," I whispered to the Mustang. He breathed along the side of my neck, and his breath smelled like sage.

I glanced back at the wagons. No one could hear me talking to the stallion. "The Kyler girls have to be called over and over for supper," I said, and I knew it sounded like a petty and ridiculous complaint. But it bothered me when they chased back and forth through the camp, giggling, when I was helping Mrs. Kyler fix supper. They had no sense. One night Hope had kicked dirt into the bean pot. Mrs. Kyler had used a spoon to get most of it out, but I could feel it gritting between my teeth when we ate.

Toby, the McMahons' little boy, was better behaved. So were all the Taylor children. The Kylers all doted on their daughters, and they weren't exactly spoiled, but they were kind of silly-headed, maybe because nothing bad had ever happened to them.

That thought bothered me. I didn't *want* anything bad to happen to them. "Maybe I'm just jealous," I said aloud, and the Mustang flicked an ear to hear me better.

I led the Mustang farther away, settling into my everyday routine of grass finding. The Mustang wasn't pulling a heavy load or working, but neither were most of Andrew's horses, and they were all getting thinner.

Every day that we traveled, grass got scarcer. A number of times we saw some kind of antelope with pronged horns at a distance.

Twice the Kyler men rode out with their guns to try to kill fresh meat for the party. The first time they came back tired and grumpy; but the second time, they came back with two of the antelope slung over their saddles.

That night everyone in the party gathered around Mrs. Kyler's fire. I could tell that she loved it, that the commotion and the laughter—and a good supper that contained no bacon—were a balm to her sore spirits. She loved having people around, she loved joking and laughing and making each one feel welcome.

My mother had been like that—always ready for company. Watching Mrs. Kyler made me miss her so badly that I had to keep myself busy to keep from crying.

I didn't want to spoil Mrs. Kyler's happy evening. She didn't have all that many now. I knew she was constantly worried about Annie, left behind in

Council Bluff with Hiram. How could she not be worried? Annie's hands had been burned so badly. And it would be a least a year before Mrs. Kyler would find out how Annie was doing—and probably closer to two years. Letters to and from the Oregon country were slow and uncertain at best.

I sent a little prayer for Hiram and Annie's welfare and wished they could have come. Annie had been right that day back in Council Bluff. Hiram was kind. He was the best sort of man—and a good friend. I missed him.

CHAPTER THREE

❧ ❧ ❧

*It is full summer now, and the grass is sparse
and dry. We do not stop even a day to rest.
There has been no shade.*

"The prairies are behind us," Mr. Kyler said one evening. "We will have nothing but hills and rocks for quite some time—and a pass through the Rocky Mountains after that."

I sighed. Rocks and ravines were all I had seen in every direction every morning for a week or more—except to the west. In that direction, the Rocky Mountains rose up out of the earth, blue and misty with distance—and with every passing day they looked bigger.

The Mustang seemed uneasy one morning,

prancing sideways as we veered off from the wagons as we always did, searching for grass. I found three or four clumps right off that still had some green blades—most was hay brittle from the summer heat. I let the Mustang graze until the wagons had rolled past, then I ran to catch up, the Mustang trotting beside me.

The lead rope, as always, was slack between my hand and the Mustang's halter. We had walked so long, so close together every day, that it was as though as soon as I *thought* about slowing down, he responded by *doing* it.

Most of the time, I didn't think twice about him being with me—in fact, it felt odd to me when he wasn't. In the evenings, sometimes, I had the strangest feeling that I had forgotten something, that something was missing, and then I would realize that it was the Mustang, off with Delia and Midnight and the rest of the horses.

I pulled in a long breath, appreciating the cool morning air as the Mustang grazed. When he had leveled the patch we were on, we ran to catch up, then repeated the process. It felt good to run, the air was almost chilly.

I watched the ground ahead of us for snakes, but I didn't see any—nor did I expect to, at least not until the sun was enough to warm their cold blood.

The day passed slowly, the sun sliding upward in the sky until the midday heat settled against the land. After our dinner stop at noon, the wagons moved through a haze of heat and dust, the oxen plodding onward as though they had forgotten any other kind of life and would plod onward until they dropped dead.

I squinted, trying to spot patches and pockets of grass, as always, but the heat made it harder to see—the air shimmered up from the ground in waves. Grass was greener and darker than the sage, but the heat blurred the colors and the shape of the land ahead.

I saw what I thought might be grass and headed toward it, following a downward slope. There was a slough, I discovered, as I got closer, marshy and wet. There was no river, not even a creek—and the ground around the slough was dry as old bones. It had to be spring-fed, the water just bubbling up somewhere close by.

I glanced up at the Rocky Mountains in the

distance as I followed along the edge of the slough. They looked a deeper blue as we got closer, darker than the sky but not by too much. They were crowned in white.

"That's snow, Miss Liddy says," I said to the Mustang as I spotted a tiny stream flowing from the earth. The water looked clear enough, and I stepped in it to cool my bare feet—then jumped backward. The water and the mud around it were icy cold!

My reaction startled the Mustang, and he shied sideways, half rearing. I stood aside, leaving the lead rope loose, waiting for him to calm down; then, when he had, I put my foot closer to the spring. I hadn't imagined it! The ground felt like frozen soil in the middle of winter, not like sun-heated earth in the hottest part of summer.

I looked back toward the wagons. I was too far away to shout and be heard. I would go tell them in a minute. But first, I wanted to explore the slough a little. What in the world could cause such icy water? I waded into the little creek. It was so cold that I began to shiver, in spite of the hot sun. In places, there was a skim of ice on the surface. It seemed impossible. I had to reach down and touch it to believe it. I drank a little of the water. It tasted a little like moss, but it was good and cold as December icicles.

The Mustang lowered his muzzle, then lifted it, as surprised as I had been. Then he took a long drink from the shallow rill, and turned to face me, nuzzling his dripping cold muzzle against my neck.

I laughed and stepped back from him. He came with me, reaching out to nibble at my hair.

"Hey!" I scolded him, still laughing. "You'd better stop that!"

He shook his mane and tilted his head, and I turned to run, knowing he would canter a stride or two, then settle back into a trot I could keep up with as he always did.

Moving easily together, the lead rope loose in my hands, the Mustang and I played along the side of the strange ice-cold slough. It was amazing to find this little bit of winter in the oppressive heat of summer. Even the soil felt cold beneath my bare feet.

The stallion seemed to feel exactly like I did, a little giddy from the strange surprise, and just plain happy to be happy...we had had so many long, weary days on the journey.

I turned suddenly, knowing the Mustang would follow my lead perfectly. He did, tossing his mane. I ran in long strides, making him extend his trot into a spanking, staccato cadence to keep up.

Then I saw the rattlesnake, coiled and still, beside a sharp rock that jutted up out of the soil. But I saw it an instant too late. My right leg was already in motion, lifting, my left knee straightening as my weight came off my foot. The snake raised its head, rattling, a sound like steam chattering a pot lid, an ugly hissing.

Time stopped for me. I knew my foot would come to earth within inches of the snake's head and there was nothing I could do about it short of learning to fly. Then, quicker that I could think, the Mustang shouldered me aside. I was thrown a few feet, far enough, landing stumbling and stunned, the lead rope no longer in my hand.

I watched, terrified, as the Mustang reared. The snake coiled tighter and lifted its head.

"No," I shouted. "Just stay away from it!" I made a grab for the lead rope, but I couldn't get close enough.

The Mustang reared again, and I had to jump back to stay clear of his hooves. He squealed and

pounded the earth a few inches from the snake—
it recoiled, slithering backward against the rock
to shelter itself. Then it coiled again and lifted its
head. It was not going to flee, it was going to fight.
I looked around, frantic to find a stick, a rock, anything to help the Mustang.

I glanced back toward the wagons. Through the
glaring heat, someone was walking toward me. Maybe
one of the Kyler men had seen the Mustang rearing. I waved both hands above my head and screamed
"Help!" Then I turned back to the Mustang.

He was rearing once more, his head tucked into
his chest, half turned, to keep one eye on the snake.
There was no doubt that his hooves could crush
the rattler—but it might manage to strike, its fangs
pumping venom into the Mustang's foreleg—before
it died. The rock it was backed up against was the
same sharp black rock we had been traveling past
for a week. If the Mustang missed by even an inch...

"Stand back!"

I whirled, startled, and saw Grover's face, flushed
from running, his eyes on the snake.

"Get back, Katie!"

I stumbled out of his way, watching transfixed

as the Mustang dropped to all fours, danced backward as the snake slithered toward him, then reared again, even closer to the rattler. Grover cocked his arm, and I saw the rock, balanced, perfectly at home in his hand. Then he threw.

The stallion was in the air, his front hooves poised to strike. The rock smashed into the snake's skull an instant before his forehooves hit it. The Mustang drove all his weight downward, one front hoof pinning the snake to the ground for an instant, then he reared again. The second time he struck at the rattler's head, hitting hard.

But it didn't matter. The snake was already dead. Grover's rock lay beside the crumpled rattler, as though it had been there through the ages, still and solid and the same color as all the rocks around it.

I turned to face Grover. I was shaking. "Thank you..." I managed. It felt like I should say something else, but I simply could not make my mind work for a long moment. I stared at the snake, its muscles still writhing, even though its life had ended.

Grover jutted his chin at the Mustang. "You better catch him."

I looked up, my heart skipping a beat when I

saw that the Mustang was a little ways off, snorting and pawing at the earth, the lead rope trailing on the ground beside him.

He was shaking, too, but with anger, not fear. His eyes were wide and wild, and he shook his mane, hard, then reared again, striking the ground as though he was imagining the fight again, convincing himself that he had won.

"It's dead," I told him, "You don't have to worry about it anymore."

He stood steady at the sound of my voice and lifted his head sharply. He watched me walk toward him. I kept talking quietly, telling him how strong and brave he was, how he had saved my life.

He came toward me, and I reached out to gather up the lead rope as he nuzzled my cheek, blowing out long, windy breaths against my skin. "It's all right now," I told him again.

Then I bit my tongue. I was talking a blue streak to the Mustang. Grover would never stop taunting me now.

"He sure does trust you," Grover said quietly.

The soft, nearly gentle tone of his voice caught me off guard. I stared at him, waiting for him to sneer, to say something mean. But he didn't. "You saved his life," I said. "I am forever grateful. If he had been bitten...if he had died..."

I couldn't finish either sentence, and Grover just ducked his head anyway. Was he trying not to laugh? I was pretty sure he would lift his chin, grin his mean grin, and start to make fun of me any second. Before he did, I wanted to explain; I wanted him to understand.

"The Mustang has been my only real friend," I managed. "You laugh when I talk to him, but he listens, Grover. He really does." I knew that sounded foolish, but I knew I couldn't do any better now or later. It was true. Grover could taunt me all he wanted. I was still grateful. He had saved my best friend's life.

Grover didn't say anything for so long that I thought he was so completely disgusted with me that he'd just turn and head back to the wagons, without saying anything at all. I started to hope he would do that, rather than make fun of me.

"I didn't mean to," he said finally.

His voice was flat, full of pain. It took me a long moment to figure out what he was talking about. He just waited until he saw in my eyes that I understood.

"I only meant to scare that cat," he said in a low, pained voice. "I never meant to kill it." He sighed. "Did you tell them it was me?"

I shook my head. "I was afraid to have you mad at me. I was afraid you'd hurt the Mustang."

His eyes were glossy with tears. "Last thing I want is to be cruel like him."

I understood what he meant instantly this time. He was talking about his father. "You aren't. You never will be."

He smiled, a thin, uneasy smile that faded, then disappeared. But he met my eyes. "Andrew Kyler said you can tell a person's heart by how they treat a horse—and how the horse treats them."

I didn't know what to say to that, so I didn't say anything.

"Can I pat him?"

I held the Mustang's lead rope tightly and nodded. "Just come up slow."

Grover walked toward us, and the Mustang stood still, then let Grover pat his neck. Grover backed away, smiling, another thin, awkward little smile.

I looked past him at the slough and remembered. I pointed. "There's a skim of ice on that
water. The ground is frozen, too."

His face went tight; he thought I was baiting
him. It was a hundred degrees out, easy, the heat
distorting the very air. "There is," I said quickly,
"there is. Just come look." I led the Mustang back
to the slough.

Grover touched the water and looked up at me,
grinning. "No one will believe us."

We gathered up as much of the ice as we could
carry and tried to get it back to show Mrs. Kyler.
It melted halfway back, all but a sliver or two. But
that was enough to get them to follow us. Most of
the party came to look, drinking the cold water out
of cupped hands, splashing their heat-flushed faces.

This was the oddest place I had ever been; impossible things had happened here. There was ice
on the water in late July, and Grover Heldon had
turned out to be sad, not mean.

CHAPTER FOUR

🐌 🐌 🐌

I could smell snake for two days until the sage finally
washed it away. We were headed toward high country.
I could scent pine trees on the wind sometimes. I traveled
as fast as the little one would let me.

week after Grover killed the snake, we
started the long climb over South Pass.
The name had made me picture a narrow gorge or
a steep-sided valley that curved between the high,
jagged peaks. But it wasn't like that at all.

South Pass was *miles* wide. It was like a giant hand
had smoothed out the mountains the way a woman
would smooth the soil in her kitchen garden before
she planted beet seed.

For a while, we could see peaks in every direction,
and the air got thin because we were so high, people

said. I noticed it some. I got out of breath quicker when the Mustang and I ran to catch up to the wagons, and at night I was so tired I felt sick.

Now that I wasn't afraid of Grover anymore, I began to notice how seldom he was with his own parents. He helped Andrew Kyler herd the stock most days, and when he wasn't doing that, he'd walk with the Taylors and help count the wheel turns to figure how many miles we had come, or he'd just walk by himself.

"We left the United States today," Mr. Taylor announced when the slow upgrade of South Pass leveled, then started downward.

Mr. Kyler rubbed his chin. "Are we past the divide?"

Mr. Taylor nodded. "Highest point is behind us now."

I wasn't sure what they were talking about at first, but, listening, I figured it out pretty quickly.

The Continental Divide was the high land that separated the rivers. In many places, it was a band of sky-piercing mountain peaks. Here it was a gentler slope. But the result was the same; rain that fell on the east side flowed east. Rain on the west side would run into the creeks and rivers that flowed west.

But no one in our party cared much about that part. This was what mattered to all of us: The Continental Divide was the boundary of Oregon country. So even though we still had a thousand miles to travel, we were in Oregon already. We all cheered and whooped that night, our voices rising with the campfire sparks into the dark sky. I have never seen stars as bright as they were in the Rocky Mountains.

The days passed, blurring as they often did as we traveled. We filled our water barrels from cold, clear creeks and walked through cooler, sweet-scented air. I had never seen a mountain before, nor a forest that went on for miles, so the whole place was like a magical land to me.

On the far side of the pass, we came to the Green River crossing. There were ferries, and we took one, each wagon paying the astounding price of sixteen dollars! It was outrageous—a man could buy an ox for that—but the river was deep, rocky, and swift, and no one counted a life cheaper than sixteen dollars. Everyone had heard too many stories of Green River drownings to try to save money.

After we crossed, we followed the parties we

could see in the distance ahead and turned south-west for a time, heading through barren hills toward Fort Bridger. I will never forget that part of our journey because a wonderful thing happened. Miss Liddy and her partners began to practice their show every evening that they had the strength to do so.

The first evening, they caught us all off guard. The sound of Miss Liddy laughing as loud and hearty as any man ever did made Mrs. Kyler and me turn to look. Miss Liddy was sprawled on the ground.

"Oh dear," Mrs. Kyler said. "Is she all right?"

I nodded. "She's laughing. I think she just stumbled or something and..." I trailed off because I noticed the big mare cantering away—no, not really away. She was cantering in a circle. Miss Liddy stood up, brushing off her trousers. She whistled and the mare slowed, then stopped and turned to face her. As usual, there was no tack at all on the mare. Miss Liddy made a gesture with her right hand, and the mare cantered back toward her again. "That'll teach me to keep up my work better!" Miss Liddy called to the men.

Mrs. Kyler and I were nearly done cleaning up supper and we stood side by side, neither of us speaking as the mare passed Miss Liddy and Miss Liddy whirled to run along beside her, leaping onto her back.

I blinked, not quite sure how it had happened. Miss Liddy had been on the ground one second, then, the next, she was riding, her knees bent at a hard angle, her bare feet set firmly on the mare's broad back—standing up.

The mare had a slow, collected canter, and she veered into in a wide, easy circle. Miss Liddy stood for a long moment, then dropped to her knees, straddling the mare, but with her legs bent backward so she was more or less kneeling. Then she stood again, spreading her hands wide, gathering herself. All at once she leapt backward, turned a summerset in midair, and landed on her feet.

There was a scattering of applause, and I realized we weren't the only ones watching. Miss Liddy bowed grandly and called out, for all to hear, "Thank you all very much. You're all welcome to come to our first show in Oregon City. I make all my mistakes in practice, of course."

Everyone laughed. I grinned at Mrs. Kyler, then turned to watch Miss Liddy go through the routine a second time. I was breathless. It was like watching an eagle fly high like they do sometimes, without flapping its wings. It looked impossible. I had never seen anything so wonderful in my life.

The next evening, we rushed around and finished our chores, both of us keeping one eye on Miss Liddy's wagons. She rode the big mare for a while more, practicing the summerset a few more times, then Mr. Le Croix took a turn.

He didn't do the summerset trick. He rode backward and sideways and leaned down off the mare to pick up a stone off the ground. He turned on his side and pretended to be asleep while the big, wide-backed mare cantered in her smooth, balanced way.

While Mr. Le Croix rode the mare, I saw Miss Liddy standing with Mr. Dillard and Mr. Swann. The men were holding odd club-shaped objects that made no sense until they began to toss them up in the air.

"That's called juggling," Mrs. Kyler said in a hushed voice, as though she might somehow startle the men if she spoke too loudly. "Have you ever seen it before?"

I shook my head, then realized she wasn't looking

at me, she was staring at Mr. Swann and Mr. Dillard as the wooden clubs flashed between them, faster and faster.

"No," I whispered, astounded. How did people learn to do such things? Who in the world had ever figured out how to do it in the first place?

Mr. Swann changed the rhythm, and Mr. Dillard followed perfectly. They reached high above their heads, then low, then spun around between catches. It was beautiful, like a dance. Mr. Le Croix dismounted and went to watch them.

Mr. Swann shouted a warning and threw Mr. Le Croix a club. In an eyeblink, the men were standing in a triangle, the clubs going round from one to the next. They each did tricks of their own, spinning, catching the clubs behind their backs, all without missing, even once.

I exhaled, feeling something I had never felt before. I didn't just want to watch all the amazing things Miss Liddy and her friends could do, I wanted to learn *how*.

I began to time my chores, rushing through supper cleanup, doing more than my usual share, just to be sure to be finished by the time Miss Liddy and the others began their evening practice. I wasn't the only one. By the second week, most of the party was hurrying through their evening work. On days when the road was rough or the weather turned bad and Miss Liddy and her friends decided not to practice, there was a dimming of spirits in every camp.

One morning, just before we reached Fort Bridger, I took the Mustang out to graze early, as usual. Without thinking much about it, my sleepy thoughts still circling aimlessly, I led him toward the rear of the wagon line. I had seen patches of good grass a ways back up the trail. I knew I would have time to let him graze before the Kylers were packed and ready to leave.

As we passed the last wagon, Miss Liddy's big mare whickered, and the Mustang answered her. His whinny brought answering nickers from Delia and Midnight, too. I smiled and patted his neck. "You're so handsome that all the lady horses think you're grand," I told him. He tossed his head and pranced a few paces.

"Morning!" Miss Liddy called. "Off to find grass for him?"

"I am," I called back without moving any closer.

Then I realized that I was standing fifty feet from her for no good reason. There hadn't been fever among her party or ours for all this time, and I was still acting as though I had to stay clear of her.

Then I realized something else. No one else was. I was the only one still behaving as though it was dangerous to be around Liddy and her friends.

Mrs. Craggett and Mrs. Taylor and the younger Kyler wives still barely spoke to them—not even Polly's mother. The rest of them had given her heck for speaking up that first day. But it had nothing to do with being afraid of fever.

I walked forward a few steps, and the Mustang moved with me. "It's so wonderful, the way you can ride," I called.

Miss Liddy smiled so broadly that it was as though the whole morning had brightened, ahead of sunrise. "Thank you, Katie!"

"Is it hard? It looks impossible." I walked a little closer so she could lower her voice.

"I remember the first time I saw someone trick ride," she said. "I was as amazed as you are." She pushed her hair back from her face. "I can tell you this. The only thing better than seeing it is doing it."

"Would you teach me?" The words were out of my mouth before I knew I was going to ask.

Miss Liddy frowned, and my heart sank.

"I know it would be an imposition," I said quickly. "None of us has but barely enough time to sleep as it is, and they say the worst part of the journey is ahead of us and—"

"No, it isn't any of that," she interrupted, raising one hand to stop me. "It is just dangerous, and I can't think why you would want to risk it. You are almost certainly going to end up with your uncle or the Kylers on a farm, and trick riding will be the last thing you need to know."

I had no answer for that, even though I searched hard inside myself to find one. "I don't care," I finally said. "I just want to learn."

She digested that for a long moment, then pointed at the Mustang. "On him?"

I was stunned to silence; I hadn't for one second thought about riding the Mustang. "No," I said quietly. "I don't want to ride him."

Miss Liddy tipped her head to one side.

I took a long breath, fighting the strange flood

of feelings inside myself. "I don't think he would want me to ride him," I said finally.

"Are you scared that he wouldn't let you?" she asked me in a gentler voice.

I nodded. I had never managed to explain it to myself, but she was right. I was afraid. What if he tried to buck me off, what if he shied and tried to get away? He trusted me. We were friends, but my trying to ride him could change that.

"Well," Miss Liddy said, "it's up to you. Can you finish chores a half hour earlier than usual?"

It took me a few seconds to take in what she had said. Then I nodded so hard I could feel my hair swing against my back.

Miss Liddy smiled. "Give me a few days. I'll let you know when we can start."

CHAPTER FIVE

❧ ❧ ❧

*We have found a good meadow, but there are too
many two-leggeds here. We are heading toward
the mountains, and I am glad. I can smell the pine trees
a little stronger each day.*

*F*ort Bridger was in the middle of a green
oasis of creeks and trees. There were twenty
tipis, leathern tents shaped like tall funnels. Indian
women and their trapper husbands lived in them,
Mr. Kyler said.

There were children everywhere, running and
laughing or somber-faced and concentrating on
work of some kind. I saw a boy no older than five
scraping the hair off what looked like deer hides.

The women were busy like we were, from early
light onward. Once, when I took our plates to the

creek to wash them properly, I knelt down, then, after I got started, I saw an Indian woman a little upstream. She held a heavy iron stew pot and waited politely until I had finished so she wouldn't muddy the water. Her eyes were merry and her mouth curved into a lovely smile. I tried to talk to her. She answered me, but in her own language. We could only smile at each other.

Mrs. Kyler bought soft leather slippers for all her granddaughters that the Indian women had made. And she bought a pair for me, too. I was so touched to have the present that I wept, and she hugged me.

Everyone stopped and rested a day or two at Fort Bridger—the Mormon party in front of us and the one behind us camped not far from our camp while we were there. But when we packed up our wagons and headed northwest, they all joined into one big company and turned south.

We all waved farewell to them. I wondered what their city would be like, if it was in a place that had forests and green grass, or the kind of dry, rocky kind of land we had seen so much of on the way to Fort Bridger. For their sakes, I hoped the salty lake hadn't killed all the trees.

I asked about letters in the post store. There were a few, all tossed into a cracker box. There was no sign of any more of mine and that was a relief. But there was no answer from my uncle Jack waiting for someone to carry east, either.

I was blue for the rest of the day. But maybe he had sent an answer two years before, and it hadn't reached me. That happened all the time, I knew.

So I stopped moping around and got my chores done early, just in case Miss Liddy wanted to start teaching me that evening—but she didn't. Everyone in her camp was kneeling, looking at the axle on one of the wagons. I saw them talking to the joiner at the fort the next morning. Mr. Le Croix and Mr. Dillard carried a new axle back to camp around noon.

That same day, I spent a long time brushing the Mustang while he stood with Delia and Midnight off to the edge of Andrew Kyler's herd. I pushed my hands up beneath his heavy mane and pressed my palms against the warmth of his coat.

I kept watching Miss Liddy and the men in her company as they changed the wagon axle. I felt scared and at first I thought I was just nervous about the trick riding. Maybe I would fall off so many times that I would have to give up. It would be embarrassing.

But that wasn't it, I admitted to myself as I left the Mustang that evening and went to lay out my bedroll beneath the Kyler's wagon. I was worrying about finding my Uncle Jack. What if I *couldn't*?

🙰 🙰 🙰

The evening after we left Fort Bridger, we camped on a wide level place with grass closer than usual and a creek nearby. Miss Liddy waved at me and gave me a little nod as she jumped down from her wagon bench. I settled the Mustang with the mares and Andrew Kyler's herd, then I worked at a furious pace, cleaning up after supper.

"You excited about something?" Mrs. Kyler asked me, smiling.

I nodded, then hesitated so long that I blushed. I didn't want to tell her. What if she tried to forbid me? It was dangerous; that was perfectly obvious.

"Miss Liddy promised…" I began, then I stalled.

Mrs. Kyler was watching me carefully. "Promised you what?"

I flushed red but could not make another word

୧ 49 ୨

come out of my mouth. It was silly—the whole camp would know. They would *watch*.

I made a weak gesture in the direction of Miss Liddy's wagons and took in a breath. "She said she would teach me."

Mrs. Kyler's eyes went wide. "To ride like that?"

I nodded, waiting for her to go get Mr. Kyler so they could forbid me. But she didn't. Instead, she looked wistful. "If I were still light and young and graceful . . ." She grinned at me. "Oh, I am jealous, indeed. Everyone will be. How in the world did you talk her into that?"

I smiled, relieved. Then I shrugged. "We were just talking, and I asked her straight out."

Mrs. Kyler was nodding. "I remember that first day, the way you two called out to each other, discovered you'd both lost your parents."

I had forgotten, but Mrs. Kyler was right. Maybe that was why Miss Liddy had agreed.

"I hoped once you got over being scared of the fever, you two might be friends," Mrs. Kyler said. "Go on. I can finish up here."

I hugged her. "I thought you would try to talk me out of it."

"Mr. Kyler will, but we'll work on him."

I smiled at her again, then started running toward Miss Liddy's wagon. They had camped a little farther off as they had been doing since they had started practicing. It took extra room for the big mare to canter in her perfect circles.

"Are you ready?" Miss Liddy said when I got there.

I stood up straight. "Yes, ma'am."

"First of all, you need to meet Genevieve."

I started. "Genevieve?" I echoed, trying to pronounce it right. "Is that the mare's name?"

She smiled. "It is. It's an old name, French, I am told. The man who raised her knew all sorts of interesting things about horse training." She gestured for me to lead the way. I walked toward their picket line. The horses were all standing quietly, grazing.

Genevieve stood so much taller than the rest that it looked odd, like a real horse had been set next to toy horses. The closer I got, the bigger she looked. When I stopped in front of her, I stared down at her hooves. They were as big as Mrs. Kyler's pie tins.

"She's big," Miss Liddy said.

Her voice was so flat and wry that it made me laugh.

"Genevieve is the most gentle creature to walk

this earth," Miss Liddy added. "She would break a leg before she stepped on me—or you. So it is your duty to protect her from having to hurt herself. Ready to work a little?" she asked. I nodded, then saw that she was talking to the mare, not to me.

We walked a little ways from camp, the big mare following Miss Liddy as she always did, without any tack at all. Once we had found a level place, Miss Liddy stopped.

"This will do," she said. "How much riding have you done?"

"Never anything like what you do," I said timidly.

She laughed her loud, mannish laugh, and I felt suddenly shy around her. As used as I was to seeing her striding around in her trousers from a distance, she was so different from any woman I had ever known that she made me uneasy this close up.

She smiled and apologized for laughing. "I meant, can you ride a horse at all?"

I nodded, then I shook my head. "I rode when I was real little, sitting on the plow horses and sometimes behind my father on his horse."

"Never alone?"

"A few times in the pasture. I was only six when..."

"And you didn't ride much after you went to live with the farm couple?"

I stared at her, caught completely off guard. I guess it showed on my face because she apologized again. "Mrs. Kyler has told me a little about you. How mean those people were. She heard it all from your friend Hiram."

I nodded, wondering why it bothered me so much to know that Hiram had talked about the Stevenses to Mrs. Kyler. "Are you all right?" Miss Liddy asked. "I didn't mean to upset you."

"I'm fine," I said, even though it wasn't quite true.

"Let's just start with a walk and see how it feels to you," she said.

I watched her position herself by the mare's side. She bent down, facing me, her hands clasped together. "Left foot. Step in my hands like a stirrup, and I will lift you. Then swing your leg over. You can hang on to her mane; she won't mind. She won't much notice anything you do, in fact. She will be listening to me."

I took a deep breath and stepped into Miss Liddy's hands and reached upward to get a handful of mane. I was afraid I would fall off before I ever got on, but I didn't. I swung my leg over the mare's back and sat, feeling like I was astride a barn roof. The mare's back felt that high and that wide.

I heard a little round of cheers from the wagons and I twisted around to look. They were all watching. I saw Grover grinning at me. I buried both hands in the mare's mane, getting even more nervous.

"Circle, Genevieve," Miss Liddy said. The mare swayed into motion, picking her own path. "Trick horses are trained to keep a steady pace and an even line, no matter what," Miss Liddy told me. "If they slow or swerve, the rider would come flying off in the middle of a stunt. So don't worry if you flop around a bit."

I sat still and tried to square my shoulders and lift my chin the way Miss Liddy did when she rode.

"Head up, but pull your shoulders down, not back," she said quietly. I obeyed and felt the difference in my posture. It made balancing a little easier, too.

"You look very nice up there," Miss Liddy said.

I felt myself blushing—I was that pleased.

"Now let go of her mane," she said. "Spread your arms. She is only going to walk. She's trained riders before; she knows you need her help."

I lifted my arms and let my fingers curl gently, my palms down.

Miss Liddy nodded. "You have been watching carefully. That's good."

I blushed again and pulled my shoulders down. There was something wonderful about sitting on top of that tall, gentle mare. I couldn't wait for the day I could stand on her back, my arms out, amazing anyone who saw me.

"Head up," Miss Liddy said, and I lifted my chin. I wanted to look as graceful as she did, to feel like I was working magic. I concentrated, focusing on every word Miss Liddy said to me and the big mare's movements. Shoulders down, head up, eyes straight ahead. It felt *wonderful*.

CHAPTER SIX

❦ ❦ ❦

The spring smelled very strange. The little one led me
close to it, but we moved away quickly. Some of the
two-leggeds drank the water, but I would not.

*T*he next week or two was hard traveling, and I
only got to practice on Genevieve twice more
we were all too tired to do much once we stopped
for the day.

There was a hill so steep the men had to line
up behind each wagon, gripping a rope, dragging
their weight to hold the wagon back, to keep it from
rolling out of control. Then they all had to walk
back up and do it over again. It was frightening,
how steep it was. Mr. Taylor said it was just called Big
Hill. I would have named it something far worse if

anyone had asked me. It took us all day to get everyone down it safely.

One morning after that we came upon something I knew I would remember forever. There was a long, narrow patch of steaming rocks—or so it looked from a distance. As we got closer, we could smell sulfur and phosphorus and we saw water spurting up into the air.

I walked the Mustang closer. The ground was hot in places under my feet, and the steam floated along the ground like some enchanted fog. People got buckets and tins and we all tasted the soda water— just to prove to ourselves that it was real, I guess. Who would ever have thought there was a place on earth where soda water just shot up out of the rocks?

We dragged into the grounds around Fort Hall tired and worn. It seemed as if we were tired most of the time, now. Even the Kyler girls had settled down. Their running and giggling was rare now at suppertime or any other time.

Fort Hall wasn't much compared to the other forts we had seen, but it was a place to rest, to feel a little safer than we did on our own. We had come so far without a guide of any kind, but now there were many fewer people on the trail with us, and sometimes we couldn't see anyone ahead of us at all. At the forts, there were usually several parties at once. Fort Hall was no different, and it was a comfort.

I asked everyone I met if they knew my uncle. No one had heard of him. I tried not to let it frighten me.

"Want to practice?" Miss Liddy called to me the second evening we were at Fort Hall.

"I do!" I called back.

Mrs. Kyler winked at me. "I'll finish up. You can clean up breakfast to pay me back."

I stuck out my hand, and we shook to seal the bargain, then I ran to make sure the Mustang was all right before I went to Miss Liddy's camp.

This was the first time we had practiced where there were other people. I hadn't been up on Genevieve's back more than five minutes before I noticed that Grover was sitting a little ways off, watching. The second time I looked, three or four boys I had never seen before had joined him.

"I want to have her canter," Miss Liddy said.

"I'm not sure I'm ready," I began, but she interrupted me, speaking quietly to Genevieve. The mare suddenly rose beneath me as she lifted her front legs and leapt forward into a canter. I sat as steady as I could, my hands gripping her mane.

"Find the rhythm of her gait," Miss Liddy reminded me. "It's like a rocking horse with her, almost."

That made me smile, but a few minutes later, I realized it wasn't a joke. The big mare lifted her front legs high, then came down smoothly with every stride.

"Head up," Miss Liddy said as Genevieve brought me around the circle again.

I lifted my head and loosened one hand from the mare's mane. Miss Liddy noticed.

"Good. Free both hands when you can. Get them up."

I wanted to say I wasn't ready again, but I didn't. I refused to look down or to think about how far I would fall if I lost my balance.

"Breathe," Miss Liddy reminded me. "She's going well for you. She has come to trust you. Just relax and lift your arms."

I loosed my grip and let my arms rise. It felt wonderful, only a little scary—I was used to the position at a walk and this wasn't too much different, not really.

"Perfect!" Miss Liddy said, and I felt my cheeks flush. "Twice more around, Katie, then I'll have her halt in front of me."

"Yes," I called back without turning my head.

"Be ready," Miss Liddy said. "When I tell her to stop, she'll turn to come toward the center of the circle, then she will slide to a halt, she won't drop back to a trot."

I steadied myself and concentrated on keeping my posture correct for the next two rounds. Then, when Miss Liddy called the command to Genevieve, I leaned with the turn and curved my back slightly when I felt her stiffen her front legs to stop. I leaned forward just enough to keep my balance as she plunged to a halt. I kept my arms up and my head high, the way I had seen Miss Liddy do it.

Grover was on his feet instantly, clapping. The boys I didn't even know shouted and cheered. Mr. Le Croix, Mr. Dillard, and Mr. Swann whooped, all of them grinning. I heard a whistle from the other side of the camp and saw Mrs. Kyler waving; past her, I saw a group of folks from another wagon company. It was obvious that they had been on their way to the fort and had stopped to watch.

For some reason, all this made me feel strangely wonderful. My eyes flooded with tears and I blushed as I swung my right leg over the mare's withers and slid down from Genevieve's wide back the way Miss Liddy sometimes did—facing out, my head high and my arms out for balance.

Genevieve lowered her head, and I reached as high as I could to pat her broad jaw. Miss Liddy was grinning. "You're a natural. I thought you might be and you are." Then she looked over my head at her companions. "If any of you have an ounce of energy, we could use traveling money." She gestured at the crowd that had gathered to watch Genevieve and me. The men got down from the wagon bench and got out their wooden clubs.

It was amazing to watch the three men juggle— really juggle, not just their practice routines. The clubs were heavy, and still they threw them high overhead, over and over, their hands flashing too fast to follow.

They stood in a triangle and tossed the clubs back and forth in an intricate pattern that changed, then changed again. Once Mr. Le Croix ended up with all the clubs, holding them in rows beneath both arms and six in each hand. The crowd laughed when he made a face. Then he tossed the clubs back out one by one. With Mr. Dillard and Mr. Swann catching them neatly, soon they were moving in a rhythmic circle again.

"It's like magic," Grover murmured. I nodded without looking away.

When they finished juggling, there was more applause, and I turned to see that the crowd had grown—there were at least two hundred people watching.

Miss Liddy stepped forward with Genevieve at her side. People gasped to see the big mare so obedient, so well trained, without a single strap or rope on her. Miss Liddy vaulted up and sat with her arms extended. Then, moving to music that only she and Genevieve could hear, they began their act. Miss Liddy was as graceful as anything as she rode standing up, with her arms out at shoulder level. Then she dropped down, threw one leg across Genevieve's withers, and sat sidesaddle at a canter. I stared. How could anyone balance well enough to do that without a saddle?

Miss Liddy rode backward, hung down to pick

up a stone from the ground, then threw it into the air. Mr. Le Croix caught it and tossed it back. She stood up again, the stone in one hand. She vaulted upward suddenly and turned a flip in the air, landing on her feet.

The people cheered and clapped, making a din that brought even more of a crowd out of the fort to see what was going on.

As the crowd noise subsided, Mr. Le Croix and Mr. Dillard began shouting at each other, spitting insults back and forth. My stomach tightened until I saw the smile on Miss Liddy's face. Looking for all the world like two men about to fight, Mr. Dillard and Mr. Le Croix circled each other. The crowd stared.

Then Mr. Le Croix drew back a fist—and the motion seemed to lift him off his own feet and set him spinning. The crowd inhaled, then I heard chuckling from a few of the men.

Mr. Swann came running to help, lifting his knees high and flailing his arms. He reached out to grab Mr. Le Croix by his shoulders and stopped the spin. Mr. Le Croix doffed his hat as though he was thanking him, then ceremoniously reached out to shake his hand. The instant Mr. Swann took it, Mr. Le Croix stepped forward and somehow lifted the much-bigger Mr. Swann off the ground and flipped him over his shoulder.

The crowd roared as Mr. Swann stood up, dusting his clothes and glowering. The mock fight went on, with both men using exaggerated gestures and pretending that gentle taps sent them flying. The crowd's laughter brought more and more people to watch.

Mr. Le Croix ran at Mr. Dillard like a furious bull. At the last instant, Mr. Dillard bent forward, and Mr. Le Croix jumped to his shoulders. Mr. Le Croix raised one finger to his lips, warning the crowd not to give him away. Mr. Dillard pretended to be confused, peering in all directions to see where Mr. Le Croix had gone. The crowd laughed so long and so hard that I thought they might never stop.

Finally, the sunset pinked the sky, and Liddy and her companions lined up to bow. Before the applause died down, they walked forward into the crowd, each one carrying his hat out upside down for people to put coins into.

As I walked back to Mrs. Kyler I could hear people joking and talking. Miss Liddy and her friends had changed a glum, weary crowd into a happy one.

Once I was back at the Kylers' wagon, I let Mrs. Kyler know I was there, then I ran to the herd and found the Mustang on the edge as usual, standing quietly with Delia and Midnight. I kissed him on the forehead, then told him about riding Genevieve.

"Did you hear people cheering? The first time?" I asked him. "That was for me."

"Katie?"

Grover's voice startled me. I turned, wondering if he was going to tease me about talking to the Mustang. He hadn't for a long time, but it probably *did* sound pretty funny to hear me talking to him like he was a person.

"Katie, do you think they would teach me?"

I looked at him. "To trick ride?"

He nodded. "Anything. I just wish I could go with them."

It took me a few seconds to understand what he was saying. "But your family—" I began.

"I know." He nodded. "My mother is sick a lot now. She needs my help." He looked up at me. "And my father would never let me go, anyway," he said. "Never."

I had no idea what to say, but he sounded so sad that I touched his arm. "I will ask Miss Liddy."

He looked so grateful that I felt awkward. "Grover, I don't know what they'll say, but I will ask, I promise." He thanked me, then ran off. I stood a long time next to the Mustang wishing things were not so hard for Grover or me, or anyone else.

The next day, I asked Miss Liddy what she thought about the men teaching Grover like she was teaching me.

"He can ask them himself, Katie," she said quietly. "I can't say what they would do. I won't put him up on Genevieve. Tell him I am sorry, but one student is all the mare and I can handle."

I told Grover that night, and he hung his head. "She didn't say they wouldn't," I repeated, "just that you should ask the men yourself."

He nodded, and I wondered if he would. He was shy, especially with adults. I had seen him taking to Mrs. Kyler a few times, but to almost no one else.

We were back in salt-dry sage country right after we left Fort Hall. The ground was rockier than anywhere we had crossed yet, dark, jagged rocks that cut my feet. I started wearing the leather Indian slippers Mrs. Kyler had bought me.

They were the best shoes I had ever owned, soft enough that I could still feel the ground, but strong enough to dull the rocks' edges.

The days were hot and dusty. I practiced riding Genevieve every evening that Miss Liddy would let me. I got better, a tiny bit each time, at holding the erect posture that made her riding so beautiful.

We crossed creeks and rivers, none so big as to be very dangerous, which was such a relief. I had heard the men talking about the Columbia River, which we'd have to cross some way or another toward the end. They compared it to the Missouri in size, but rougher, with circular currents and no ferry boats except tied-together Indian canoes. I tried not to think about it.

After one river crossing—no one seemed to know the name of the river—we passed a cutoff trail, a pair of shallow-rutted tracks, heading south into the California country. It was a faint trail compared to the one we were on. I saw Mr. Silas staring down it as we rolled past.

The oxen plodded slowly forward in the midday heat, and I spotted wagons in the distance. Some had turned off for California. They were headed southwest, raising so much dust that I couldn't see how many there were.

I hadn't met anyone who was going to California and I wasn't sure what drew them there instead of Oregon. There must be some reason.

I suddenly thought about my uncle Jack. Maybe he had started out for Oregon and had gone to California instead. Maybe that's where his family was—hundreds of miles south. Would he have gone to join up and fight in the war?

The thought made my skin prickle. I didn't think he would have done that without letting my mother know, but I had to admit it was possible. It would explain the returned letter at Fort Laramie.

My eyes filled with tears. How was I supposed to know what to do? How was I supposed to find him? I stepped back and hid behind the Mustang as we walked closer to the wagons so no one would see me crying.

I had been so sure that I would find my uncle Jack in Oregon country and I still thought I would be able to. But the truth was, back home in Iowa, I had never realized how big the Oregon country was—and I had never once imagined or understood how hard or how long the journey would be.

There was an enormous difference between thinking about walking two thousand miles and actually walking each mile, one by one.

As always, the Mustang kept turning to nuzzle at my face and shoulder when he heard me sniffling, trying to hold back the tears.

I tried, but the tears came anyway and rolled down my cheeks. Hurrying, I led the Mustang even farther away from the wagons and found a swath of good grass off the trail.

I stopped, and he dropped his head to graze. I stood so the Mustang was between me and the wagons and gave up on fighting the tears. I just wanted my family back. I wanted to see my mother and my father. I wanted to play with my beautiful little sister. I leaned against the Mustang's shoulder and just plain sobbed. As he had since the beginning, the Mustang stood still, reaching around to touch me with the velvet-soft skin of his muzzle, nudging at my shoulder.

I didn't start after the wagons until I was finished crying. I didn't want Mrs. Kyler to see me coming undone. She had enough to worry about with her own big family.

As we got close to the end of the wagon line, the Mustang lifted his head suddenly and drew in a long, shuddery breath. I let out the lead rope to allow him to shake his mane and prance a little to one side.

"Do you smell something?" I asked him. "Is there something dangerous up ahead?"

He shook his mane again. Then he danced a half circle and I had to follow him.

I held the lead rope without pulling on it. Something was really upsetting him. "What is it?"

He stamped a back hoof, hard. Then he whinnied, a high, squealing call.

"What is it?" I asked him again. "Oh, how I wish you could just talk to me."

He blew out a sharp breath and whinnied once more. We were close enough to Andrew Kyler's stock that the mares heard him and answered. But then, a few seconds later, I heard another whinny, from the other direction.

Indians? Trappers? It wasn't anyone driving any kind of a wagon, that much was sure. No wagon could make it up or down the hills on either side of the trail. Even the trail itself was full of rocks that the wooden wagon wheels jolted up and over.

I walked faster, and then ran until we caught up with the wagons. I kept my eye out for riders coming out of the rough country on all sides of us for the rest of the day, but no one did.

The next day I heard the whinny again when I was searching for grass for the Mustang. This time he turned, pulling me along with him, and squealed a long, high-pitched call, his head so high I had to reach up to catch hold of the halter. He squealed again and I heard a distant answer. It was then that I saw the horses through the trees, flashing past at a gallop, barely visible in the distance.

They were galloping in a group, strung out behind a big-boned gray. Behind them ran a horse that looked a lot like the Mustang. He had a thick, black mane that streamed out behind him. I waited to see who was herding the animals along, half expecting to see Indians. But the horses passed and disappeared, and even though I stared, I couldn't spot a single rider. It took me such a long time to figure it out that I blushed with embarrassment when I finally did. No one was herding them. They were wild.

I looked at the Mustang, at his arched neck. His eyes were as bright and alive as I had ever seen them. His nostrils were flared wide as though he had been running. For an instant, he surged forward, pulling at the rope so hard that I stumbled and nearly fell, hanging on to it. Then he looked back at me and slowed again, and I caught up.

I patted his neck, and we walked on together as we had been doing for months. I found a good patch of grass, and he lowered his head and ate hungrily. My stomach was fluttery. I would have to be more careful. If he ever saw wild horses up close, he would probably try to follow them.

CHAPTER SEVEN

🙦 🙦 🙦

The rocks here are sharp, and the oxen go even slower than
before. The little one and I sometimes run a little
and I am grateful. In the cool of the mornings, I long
to gallop, but I know the little one could not keep
up. I heard a stallion and scented his mares. There are
horses here that do not walk with two-leggeds.

Not long after that we came upon the Snake
River. It was so beautiful to see water in the
middle of that strange and broken countryside, the
river curving in a long sinuous path across the broken,
rocky land. Its surface was smooth as a gray-green
looking glass on the cloudy day when we came over
a rise and saw it below us.

The river was some distance from the trail at first,
then the wagon tracks led us closer to the banks. The
river had worn away the soil to form steep-sided
bluffs. We saw many strange sights as we went. There

was one stretch of bluffs on the far side of the river that spouted roaring springs that flumed enormous waterfalls straight out into the air, splashing downward to fall into the river below. It was as if an underground river ended there, joining one that ran aboveground.

One fine morning, as it was just barely beginning to turn light, we all heard splashing in the water. We stopped our morning chores and turned to look. In the dusk we could just make out blurred silver arcs—fish were jumping!

Andrew and two of his brothers rigged up netting, using twine from the Taylors' goods. By midmorning, they had soaked themselves and caused their wives hours of worry, but they had caught ten of the magnificent fish.

"Salmon!" Mr. Kyler said happily when he saw them. "I've heard about this kind of fish."

No one even suggested traveling on until the fish were cooked and eaten. It was heaven, after all the months of beans and bacon, to eat the delicate, pink fish meat.

Mr. Taylor and Mr. Heldon made hooks from old wire corset stays that Mrs. Kyler gave them.

They used twine for line and baited the hooks with chunks of bacon. The salmon didn't seem to be as tired of it as we were, because they took the bait and were pulled in, hand over hand, to the rocky banks. This was much easier than stringing nets, and all the men endeavored to make hooks and lines.

We ate salmon whenever we could, and it was delicious every time. The bacon we carried had been half-rancid for weeks in spite of being salted until it was nearly intolerable and stung our mouths.

But even though we got a welcome change in our meals, our stock did not. One night after supper, Miss Liddy pulled me aside. She looked sad.

"I want to stop the lessons for a while."

I felt my heart sinking, but I knew why. "We shouldn't work Genevieve at all, probably," I said aloud.

Miss Liddy nodded unhappily. "She's losing flesh. They all are. This cursed sage," she said, taking a sideward kick at a clump of the gray-green plant, "doesn't nourish like grass does." She shook her head. "And you can tell they hate it."

It was true. "The Mustang curls his lip—and he is eating less," I told her.

"They only eat it because there isn't much choice," Miss Liddy said. "Ever wonder if you made a mistake by coming?" she asked me.

It caught me off guard. "Sometimes," I admitted. "If I can't find my uncle..." I trailed off because I couldn't think about it without feeling physically sick.

"Oregon City will have enough people to give our show," Miss Liddy said quietly. "So we'll make some money, enough to winter on, I expect." She pushed her hair back. "Come spring we might head south to Mexico City if the war is over and travel is easy. I've never seen Alta California. I want to."

I was astonished at the idea of her going where the war was being fought now, of talking about traveling an inch farther than we had to. I was also fascinated by the idea. Mexico City! What was it like just to go places because you wanted to see them?

"I'd like to travel one day," I said quietly.

Liddy nodded. "Then you should."

I looked at her. "The Kylers promised to get me to Oregon and help me find Uncle Jack," I told her. "I can't imagine that he'd ever let me go traveling on my own."

She smiled gently. "Circus life is hard work. And you're right, most people wouldn't let a girl your age go traveling. I did, but there wasn't anyone to tell me not to."

"Liddy? We need your help here!"

It was Mr. Le Croix, shouting from across the camp. She waved at him to let him know she'd heard, then she kissed my forehead, her hands gripping my shoulders. "You are going to have a fine home, Katie. You are a wonderful girl, and they will be lucky to have you."

I watched her walk away, feeling odd. The wagons would all separate when we got to Oregon City, I knew. The Kylers, the McMahons, the Heldons, the Craggetts, and the Taylors would be looking for land, I was sure. Who knew what Mr. Silas and his friends were thinking? They didn't seem like farmers to me. I wondered where we might all end up—if we would ever see one another again.

It made me sad to think I might not ever see Mrs. Kyler again. She had been so good to me. She was so funny, so patient; I knew my mother would have loved her.

I felt tears seeping into the corners of my eyes,

and I turned away, walking fast. I needed to graze the Mustang. Lately, no matter how hard I worked to find grass, he was getting thin.

Maybe he was sorry he'd allowed me to lead him all this way. Maybe he would have been better off if he'd just kept going that time he'd run off. The thought startled and hurt me, and I pushed it aside. I took good care of him, and I always would.

I led him away from the wagons, and after a half mile or so, I spotted a patch of grass that still had a little green in it. The Mustang veered toward it when I did, without so much as a tug on the lead rope. He walked beside me, not behind me, as always. It wasn't like I was leading him. We were just walking together.

CHAPTER EIGHT

❧ ❧ ❧

The river was wide and deep, and the water was cool.
It was hard swimming—the current was very strong.
We need to find better grass. The mares are weary
from all this travel and need to rest. The two-leggeds
must know this, but still they travel onward.

*M*rs. Kyler was cheerful as we cleaned up
after supper every evening. But she was
quieter than she had been a month before. She
looked tired, too. As we walked along the rutted trail
beside the Snake River, the wagons creaking and
moaning over the rocks, I began to realize that a
lot of people weren't doing all that well.

Poor Mrs. Heldon had terrible stomachaches
that made her double over with pain, and sometimes
she had to vomit. She would walk away from camp,
but we could hear her, and we all felt sorry for her.

I noticed Grover doing the cooking for his father most mornings and at supper, too. His mother was lying down in the wagon every moment she could.

Andrew's wife, Hannah, was pregnant again—the rest of us could finally see what she must have known in Council Bluff. She looked nearly faint on the hottest days.

Mr. and Mrs. McMahon had lost their plump faces. She was thin as a scarecrow. Their little boy, Toby, was often weepy and whining, and I saw blood on his chin now and then.

For some reason, a number of people had dark, tender gums that bled when they ate. Andrew Kyler had had his left hand bound up in cotton rags for weeks—he had cut himself, and it hadn't yet started to close and heal.

Those among us who weren't hurt or sick were just plain tired. I was. Polly and Julia and Hope usually lay in one of the wagons reading to one another at night right after supper. I barely noticed them anymore, they were so quiet.

Mr. Kyler seemed tired almost all the time now, dawn to dusk. He looked older than he had when Hiram and I had met him, too. I heard him sigh a hundred times a day. And poor, pale Mary Taylor was too weak to walk to supper most nights.

Her father would carry her, setting her gently on an overturned apple box so she could get out from beneath the dirty wagon canvas and sit with us under the wide sky for a half hour or so each evening.

Mr. Silas and his friends kept farther and farther apart from the rest of us. They had never been much for socializing, but now they kept to themselves so much it was rare that any of them spoke to one of us.

I heard them arguing now and then, if I grazed the Mustang close to their wagon. From what I could gather, Mr. Silas had talked the others into coming, and they were all beginning to question whether what he had told them about the wonderful land of Oregon was true. One of them kept saying they should have turned off to go to California instead of heading into these treacherous mountains.

I led the Mustang away before they could notice me. The truth was, a lot of the families were having similar doubts and similar talks. We were all just so tired.

All the weary way to Fort Boise we traveled across dry country littered with sharp, dark rocks that gritted and ground at the wagon wheels. We stayed there only a day. As hot as it was, the menfolk were worried about being in the Blue Mountains when the snows began, so we pushed on. I asked after my uncle, but again, no one had ever heard of him.

The sun had felt like an enemy all through August, and, as we passed into September, the hot days ran one into the next. The country was so rough, so barren, that if the Snake River hadn't been there, we would never have made it through.

Finally, we got a few cloudy days and some relief from the heat. But the rain, when it came, pelted down in a flood and soaked us all, leaving the trail a mud mire. There was lightning, too, so loud and bright it seemed fit to crack the earth in two. Over and over it hit near enough to shake the very ground. The Mustang was terrified, and so was I. We stood by the wagon close together. He was trembling.

"Katie Rose, get inside!" Mrs. Kyler shouted at me more than once.

I pretended that I couldn't hear over the pounding of the rain, and she finally gave up. I knew she meant well and was only trying to take care of me, but I felt safer standing outside with the Mustang than

I ever felt huddled inside the canvas-topped wagon—
and he needed my comfort as much as I needed his,
I was sure.

It rained most of the night. Around midnight,
Mr. Kyler brought me a piece of canvas to wear like
a shawl and his own hat. I was already soaked, but it
helped some, and I was grateful. I leaned against the
side of the wagon, and I guess I fell asleep standing up.

At sunrise the next morning, I was startled awake
by a long, eerie, wailing sound. It was Mrs. Taylor.
Sometime during the long, violent storm, Mary Taylor
had gone outside the wagon for some reason. She had
been unable to climb back in and she was soaked to
the bone, shivering and feverish. None of the Taylors,
deep in an exhausted sleep and deafened by the rain
on the canvas, had heard her.

I could see the anguish in Mrs. Taylor's eyes from
that morning onward, and I felt sorry for her. She
and her husband took such good, tender care of
Mary. They were as loving as two parents could be,
and it broke their hearts to have failed her.

Not long after that, we had to cross the Snake
River. There were three islands in the river at the
crossing. We camped and watched another party

go over, and while we were camped, a big party of wagons caught us up and passed, going south rather than crossing the river where we were.

I heard some of the men calling to the other party, asking what they knew about the trail ahead. That set the menfolk to debating. It was another hard decision, like all the rest. Some wanted to wait and cross farther north. The men in the party that had gone past had thought it might be easier farther on.

Mr. Silas wanted to build rafts to float the wagons. Mr. Kyler liked the idea, but everyone knew it would take three or four days to cut trees and lash the logs together. And there weren't many trees close to on this side of the river. It'd mean dragging them with our already tired oxen.

I noticed Liddy's three companions joining in as the decision was made. Mr. Swann was strongly for crossing. We'd had cloudy afternoons the past two days, and, if it rained again, the river could rise. Mr. Dillard kept pointing out that the islands would let us cross in the wide spot, where the water would be at least a little less deep.

It became a shouting match. Mr. Le Croix argued

one side, then switched to the other, then back. Andrew Kyler liked the idea of the stock being able to rest on each island, but he wasn't sure about anything else.

In the end, we crossed. I think the men were too tired to keep arguing about it. It took the whole day, what with figuring the best way, then recaulking the wagons so they would float better, easing the load for the oxen to pull as they swam across the deepest places. We spent hours repacking, deciding who would ride where and how to get everyone over the water. It was past noon before we ever started.

I rode with Mr. and Mrs. Kyler again. The Mustang would stay with the mares and swim over, with the Kyler boys herding the whole bunch.

Mr. Kyler led the way, and I was glad. The only thing worse than crossing rivers was *waiting* to cross rivers, staring at the water, worrying. Mr. Kyler shouted and whipped the oxen forward, forcing them into the water until it was deep enough to swim, then he reined them toward the first island and shouted encouragement as they headed toward it.

I thought the current might push us too far downstream, but Mr. Kyler had figured it right. The wagon bumped against the bottom, and Mr. Kyler started a second fit of shouting and whip snapping to urge the oxen up out of the water and on up the bank.

Once we were on level ground, Mrs. Kyler gave me a quick hug, then got down to walk alongside, watching the wagons behind, concerned for her family. I got down to walk beside her, keeping an eye on the Mustang, still on the far shore with the rest of the horses.

Mr. Kyler guided the oxen the length of the little spit of land, then let them stand and rest for half an hour before he drove them into the water a second time. While we waited, two more wagons had come across. Mrs. Kyler went to check on Hannah, then came back. Hannah had insisted on driving her wagon while Andrew drove the stock as usual, even though her pregnancy made Andrew nervous and protective.

Andrew had the stock spread out and grazing. He would bring them across last. Mrs. Kyler and I got back up on the wagon bench. It made me uneasy, as always, to be separated from the Mustang, and I fidgeted so much leaning out to look back that Mrs. Kyler reached out and took my hand.

Finally, Mr. Kyler popped the whip and swam the oxen across an even deeper channel to the second island. The current was strong, and I gripped the wagon seat with both hands, staring at the rushing water.

We waited again, this time for nearly an hour. Then we led the way to the third island. It was the smallest, and it had steep banks. The wagon jolted, and I hung on to the edge of the driver's bench as the oxen staggered out of the water and onto dry land again. Mr. Kyler rested the team an hour or so before he asked the oxen to swim the last stretch back to solid ground.

They heaved and blew as they swam the last channel, their breath rasping when they touched bottom and began to pull again. The instant the wagon halted, I jumped down and ran back to watch the rest of the wagons come across. All came fine, except the Taylors'. The current tumbled it over and we all stood helpless, watching the oxen struggle to keep their muzzles above water, fighting their wooden yokes and the harness. I could see Mr. Taylor clinging to one wheel. His wife was washed downstream, but she wasn't far from the bank, and Charles Kyler jumped in to save her. Their other children hung on to the wagon and were dragged to safety when the oxen stumbled up onto the bank.

The one no one could save was poor Mary. Weak and ill with the fever she'd caught in the rain, she had been in the back of the wagon and had been drowned. From the instant we saw her limp form in her father's arms, the whole party went silent. He carried her alongside the wagon while Mrs. Taylor drove. Both looked stricken, and we all just watched them come ashore, unable to say or do anything to help them.

Last across were Andrew and his brothers with the horses. The Mustang swam at the rear as he usually did, a little off to one side, Delia and Midnight just in front of him. It was a wide, deep river, and I held my breath, but the horses all came across safe to the first island.

Andrew let them blow and shake and graze until they had all caught their breath and rested a little, then he brought them on across to the second island, then the third.

I ran toward the Mustang as he waded out. "Mary died," I whispered to him, and somehow that made it real. My eyes burned. I was standing too close when he shook the water from his coat. He spattered my dress.

I turned to walk beside him up the bank and saw Grover watching me. He had dark circles beneath his eyes. I had barely spoken to him lately. He had been busy dawn to dark doing almost all his mother's chores as well as his own. I was pretty sure her stomach had gotten worse.

"Poor Mary," he said.

I nodded and sighed. "Poor Mary."

Grover walked a little closer, keeping one eye on the Mustang. The stallion flicked his ears back and forth. I wondered if he remembered that Grover had killed the rattlesnake.

"She was always so nice to me," he said.

I nodded. It was impossible for me to talk much about Mary just then. I think he felt the same because he just nodded, then bit at his lower lip for a long time. "Mr. Swann showed me a little juggling trick," Grover said finally. "I've been practicing." He fished in his pockets and pulled out three round stones as we walked up the bank and followed the slow, sad parade of people in front of us.

"Look." Grover tossed one stone in the air, and caught it in his other hand. Then he tossed a second one. Then, for a few seconds, he had all three stones in the air at once before he got mixed up and dropped them.

"It looks hard," I said.

He nodded. "It is."

"How is your mother feeling?" I asked, patting the Mustang's neck.

Grover shrugged. Then his eyes met mine for an instant. "She can't eat. I think she might be dying." He said it so quietly that, for a moment, I wasn't sure I'd heard him right. But I could see in his eyes that I had.

I didn't know what to say. I just reached out and touched his hand. I thought he might talk about it more, but he didn't. I wanted desperately to say something to help. I took in a breath, and I even opened my mouth, but no words came out. Everything that formed in my mind sounded empty and useless in the face of Mary's death, and what he had just told me.

"I'm so sorry," I finally managed. My voice sounded stiff and brittle. But he wasn't listening to me; he was turning away. He walked slowly, like he had forgotten I was there. I watched him pass his parents' wagon and head off into the trees. I said a little prayer for him, then added one for Annie and one for Hiram.

Even though there was a grave to dig, no one wanted to go any farther than we had to after the exhausting river crossing, so we camped about a half mile from the river. I could see the oxen's legs trembling with fatigue as Mr. Kyler unhitched them.

They were thin and exhausted, and it scared me. What would all the families do if the oxen gave out? We could only hope to hit better grass country soon. The horses in Andrew's herd were all looking rough. Midnight's ribs stood out. Delia had kept her weight a little better.

The Mustang still had a bit of flesh over his ribs as well, but that was only because I did nothing all day except find him little clumps and patches of grass.

The women set to making camp in silence. The men found a place to dig a grave. The grave digging was terrible hard work, hampered by mud and sprinkling rain—and the rock. I stood back through most of it, busying myself with finding grass for the Mustang and with helping Andrew gather up the stock. He was stumble-tired, had gotten even less sleep than I had.

Once the grave was deep enough for decency, I heard Mrs. Taylor sing a hymn, her voice shaking and weak, but brave. Then Mr. Taylor read from the Bible. They had wrapped their daughter in a quilt and buried her in it. I could not watch the whole time. The feelings that stirred inside me were more painful than I could bear.

In the morning, the oxen walked slowly as we started off in the chilly predawn dusk. "How much farther do we have to go?" I asked Mr. Kyler when the Mustang and I came past his wagon. I smiled, waiting for him to tell me Oregon City was around the next bend.

"I don't know for certain, Katie," he said slowly. "I'd say three, four hundred miles."

I could only stare at him, it surprised me that much. He saw my reaction and gathered the reins in one hand so he could reach out and pat my head.

"It's a hard road, no doubt about it," he told me. "But we have to get along it now quick as we can to beat the snow. No time to rest."

I nodded and tried to smile at him; he looked so worn out that it worried me.

"Snow would be about the only thing that'd stop us now, though," he said, and chuckled as though he had said something funny.

I smiled and nodded. "It won't snow," I said, just to be cheerful, too.

He shrugged. "It will or it won't; no way to know. I hope not." He looked up at the sky. It was clear overhead, but there were a few clouds on the northern horizon. "Storms probably come in from the north out here, or maybe the west, coming in off the ocean."

I waited for him to say something more, but he didn't. I finally gave him a little wave and angled the Mustang off the rutted trail, to look for grass. I could tell Mr. Kyler was truly worried.

When I found a patch of dry, leathery grass, I stopped and the Mustang dropped his head to graze. I leaned against him and he lifted his head, turning to nuzzle my face, his mane falling like a shawl across my shoulders. I was so tired of traveling. I was so worried about so many things. But I didn't cry. I couldn't. Maybe a person had only so many tears in her, I thought. Maybe I had run dry. But, it turned out not to be true.

Later, walking some distance from the others, I cried for Mary and for myself and for Annie's poor burned hands and for Grover and for the mare that had broken her leg and for all the weary world.

The Mustang nuzzled at me and walked more slowly than he usually did, matching his pace to mine for the rest of the day. I put one foot in front of the other, and that was hard enough.

CHAPTER NINE

❧ ❧ ❧

I smell snow in the wind sometimes. It is out there, waiting
for its time to come. I would not want to be caught in
these rocky pine forests by the snow. The two-leggeds are
traveling hard. They must know the danger.

We were in the Blue Mountains now—the
part of the trail everyone had always said was
the worst. It was. There was one grade so steep that
I stood at the bottom and held my arm out, sight-
ing along my hand at the top of the rise. My elbow
touched my ear, it was that steep!

It took us two terrible days to get all the wagons
up. We hitched twelve oxen to each wagon. Even so,
it was hard.

At the top, the men would rest and unhitch one
team, then start back down, driving the six oxen

ahead of them. We went on that way until dark, each team pulling twice.

A few days later we came to another hill almost as steep, and it slanted side to side as well. Each wagon was double teamed again. We all lined up on the low side and pushed against the wagons, palms flat against the wooden bed rails. We had to walk sideward, crisscrossing our legs with each step, shoving with all of our strength to keep the wagons from crashing down the mountainside.

Every hand was needed. I left the Mustang with Andrew's herd and the mares so I could do my part. The Taylors' youngest son watched the stock with Grover's mother and little Toby. The boys were seven and five, and Mrs. Heldon could barely stand, but Mr. Kyler was so afraid that one of the wagons would tilt and wreck, rolling downward, that he asked everyone to help. Mrs. Heldon rode up in the last wagon, and Toby and I held the stock until Andrew and Charles Kyler could get back down.

A few days after that, there was a steep, rocky downgrade, and we used the heavy ropes as make-shift drags and brakes as we had before. One place was so steep that we had to unload every single-bingle wagon, lower it down by rope over a rock shelf, then lower the goods down to repack. One ox broke a leg and had to be shot. It was awful.

Mr. Silas butchered the poor animal and we all ate fresh meat for a few days. I was ashamed that we had driven the poor animal to its death, but like everyone else I was starved for fresh meat. Everyone's bacon was rancid, plain and simple. It stank. But everything else was long gone.

I had a dream one night, about eating a salmon supper. When I woke up I was so disappointed that it had been only a dream that I nearly wept.

One chilly morning, we woke to a ground frost that coated the pines and crackled beneath our feet when we started off. We had followed a deep rutted trail all the way. But more and more we were sure that whoever had run wagons down to— and over—that rock ledge had been lost. And so were we. We all kept walking, and no one talked about it much. I was grateful. Talking about it would have only made it worse.

We saw deeper ruts on a road we came upon, and so we turned down it. That must have brought us back on course, because we saw wagons ahead of us two days later. And Mr. McMahon had a name in his guidebooks for the big, lovely valley we came into shortly thereafter.

Grand Round was a pretty place. There was a wide valley surrounded by country as pretty as anything we had seen in the Rocky Mountains. The soil was dark and smelled like farmland. And the hillsides were covered with tall, stately pine trees. It was beautiful, and everyone slowed to breathe in the soft air and gaze at the hillsides.

I was walking the Mustang beside the wagon. "You have to wonder why this isn't far enough," Mrs. Kyler said, looking around. She climbed down off the wagon, jumping off the step as the oxen went on. Mr. Kyler frowned and watched to make sure she'd landed safe, then turned back to face the road ahead of the wagon.

"Why should we go another step?" Mrs. Kyler asked the sky, stretching, then pressing her hands against her back.

I nodded and stopped with her. It was a wonderful place. Even the air was fine, scented with the pine needles. I could see two creeks, looking down the wide valley.

The Mustang tossed his head and pranced a little. I pulled him off to one side. I shivered, and Mrs. Kyler noticed.

"You have a heavy jacket?"

I nodded.

"Does it still fit?"

I nodded again. "I think it will. Hiram bought it too big. I need to get it out, I guess."

Mrs. Kyler went silent for a while, and I wished I hadn't mentioned Hiram. Thinking about him could only make her think about Annie. All the hard and weary miles behind us lay between her and her daughter.

Mrs. Kyler finally turned to look at me. "I suppose we'll have to keep on all the way to Oregon City."

I smiled at the resigned tone of her voice. "I suppose we will."

She sighed and pressed her hands against her back again. "The menfolk talk about Oregon City like it is heaven on earth."

We both pulled in a deep breath at the exact same moment, then let it out as if we had counted ready, set, sigh! It made us laugh, and the laughter helped us keep walking. Sheer habit kept us going, too.

We were so used to it that it was hard to imagine stopping sometimes.

A few days later two men on horseback caught up to us. They had been visiting friends near Fort Boise and were on their way home to Oregon City. Mr. Kyler called a greeting, and they reined in. He handed the reins to Mrs. Kyler, then turned sideward and jumped off the bench without reining the oxen in. They plodded onward. Mr. Kyler lifted his knees high for a few steps, getting the kinks out of his muscles, then strode along, talking, walking alongside the strangers.

I was saw Mr. Taylor climbing down, too, then Mr. McMahon and Mr. Le Croix. Within a few minutes, all the wagons were still moving and all but three had women at the reins: Mr. Swann and Mr. Dillard kept driving Miss Liddy's second and third wagons, of course, and Mr. Silas had passed the reins to one of his men. No one stopped. We were all afraid to stop—we were racing the snow.

The men coming from the rear of the line trotted past, then fell in beside Mr. Kyler, listening and talking.

The men stopped when we did for noon dinner,

the sun straight overhead. They had their own food, and I saw that Mrs. Kyler was relieved. We had little to offer besides smelly salt bacon.

I led the Mustang close. "Do any of you gentlemen know a Mr. Jack Rose?" I asked quietly. They all glanced up, shook their heads, then looked back into their plates. My heart was beating wildly, as it always did when I asked that question.

"You get that horse from around here?" one of the men called after me.

I turned, puzzled.

"There are wild ones in this country that look like that. Folks say they're from the Spaniards' horses that got set loose or lost a few hundred years ago."

"I brought him from Iowa," I said, and watched the man's brows lift. I didn't want to explain anything to him. I didn't want to talk at all. I crossed the little clearing where we'd stopped. I found some low, tough-bladed grass for the Mustang and he grazed while I swallowed my disappointment and tried to reason with myself. I would find someone who did know my uncle Jack eventually. I would. I had to. I shoved the thoughts aside and focused on what the man had said about the Mustang.

"Was your great-great-great-great-granddaddy from Spain?" I asked him. The idea pleased me. It seemed fitting that a horse as wonderful as the Mustang had come from somewhere magical like Spain.

As the Mustang grazed, one of the men drew a map in the dirt. Our menfolk crowded around, and I saw them nodding. They had decided something. I walked the Mustang back to the wagon and stood beside Mrs. Kyler.

"We're going to Whitman Mission," Mr. Kyler said, coming back once the men had ridden on. He climbed up onto the wagon and Mrs. Kyler handed him the reins. "This road bypasses the place, but we've decided to take an extra day to get there and back."

Mrs. Kyler looked astonished. "Why, if we don't have to? Why not go straight on?"

He looked at her out of the corner of his eye. "They have crops. Carrots, potatoes, squash..."

"Squash," she echoed, and my mouth flooded with saliva.

The Whitman Mission was a neat, tidy place, and the Whitmans had made a regular paradise out of it. There were Indians, polite men who seemed comfortable enough with the Whitmans, both Mr. and

Mrs., and with us. They stared at the Mustang, though, so I kept back a little. One of the Indian men walked closer and pointed at the corrals, then back at the Mustang. I followed his gesture. Standing in the corral was a mare that could have been the Mustang's dam. She had the same dark honey coat and a black mane that fell thick and heavy down her neck.

I nodded, to let the Indian man know I understood and was glad to know there were horses like the Mustang here. I showed Andrew, and he bargained with the man who owned the mare, but she wasn't for sale. "I'd buy that stallion from you," the man said, spotting the Mustang. "We don't see many of the wild ones and almost never a stallion. They never tame down unless you catch them as colts."

Andrew shook his head. "He's not mine, but I can tell you he isn't for sale." The man shrugged and walked away.

The Whitman Mission was like a well-tended garden. They had squash and apples and even some good wheat flour that they would have given to us as gifts—but most people gave them something in barter or a few coins.

The fresh food tasted like heaven to me. Mrs.

Kyler made the squash into a soup that lasted three days. She tied the lid tight onto the pot with twine every morning so it couldn't slop much when the wagon lifted, then crashed down again as the wheels rolled over rocks.

I managed to get save a bit of the squash rind, and I fed it to the Mustang. He ate it with his eyes closed, like my mother used to drink her hot chocolate on Christmas Day.

Almost everyone seemed to gain a little health back every day from the food. We badly needed it. The Blue Mountains seemed to be determined to take the last bit of our strength.

Mrs. Heldon had been bedridden for some time, unable to eat at all. As we headed down the steep, rocky road, she got jostled and shaken, and we all heard her cry out now and then.

Grazing the Mustang one morning, I saw Grover helping her climb out of the wagon. She looked tiny and thin, like a sickly child. Neither she nor Grover noticed me, and I am ashamed to say I was relieved that I wouldn't have to call out a greeting and try to sound cheerful. I am ashamed because two days later she passed away, and I never had another chance to say anything to her at all.

We stopped for a few hours to dig a grave. Grover walked back and forth, gathering rocks and piling them on the little patch of broken earth that covered his mother. His father stood stock-still beside the grave, his hair a wild halo around his head.

I had left the Mustang with Andrew's herd, but I still stood back from the others. I watched, knowing I should say something to Grover, that I was the one, out of all of us, who should be able to say something to him. But I couldn't.

Staring at the mound of earth, listening to Mr. Kyler read from the Bible, I was lost in memories of my own parents' funeral and the weight of those memories very nearly crushed my heart. I swayed on my feet, biting at my lip, determined not to cry. My loss had no place in this wilderness beside the Oregon Trail. Poor Grover was in the first wounded day of his own grief. He had become my friend, and this was his time to cry, not mine. I stood, fidgeting, while Mr. Kyler was reading a Bible passage.

Then, on impulse, I picked up a rock so big I could barely carry it and walked, stiff-legged, to the grave. I set it down, then went to fetch another.

Grover shot me one grateful look, and I knew I had done the right thing, maybe the only thing.

Together we carried enough rocks to half cover the grave before the adults got done with their praying and Bible reading and joined in. The men carried bigger stones than we could, of course. Mr. Heldon carried a few rocks, then stood back, his face bleak and cold as morning ashes.

Mr. Taylor, Mr. McMahon, and Mr. Silas found a big black stone the shape of a wind blown storm cloud, flat on one side. Sweating and straining, they rolled and dragged it across the clearing. Then others took over and heaved at it, finally positioning it at the top of the grave for a headstone. By the time Mr. Kyler called out for everyone to get ready to go, the whole grave was well mounded with rock. Grover was still working, his eyes down.

As the wagons lurched into motion and Grover's father guided his oxen back onto the trail, I lagged behind. I kept an eye on Grover as I went to get the Mustang. When I came back, he still hadn't left the graveside. His father had taken his usual place in the line of wagons and was well ahead; he seemed to have forgotten Grover entirely.

I saw Mrs. Kyler leaning out to see around the canvas wagon cover. I waved at her and gestured toward Grover. She waved back and I knew we understood each other.

As I came closer, I saw that Grover was holding a fist-sized rock, balancing it in his hand. He looked up when he heard the Mustang's hoofbeats. His eyes were empty of everything. I wondered if I had looked the same way. He swung around, his arm tracing a wide arc, the stone leaving his hand with all the strength in his body, all the violence of this pain.

I stood with him, listening to the sound of the rock as it passed between two pine trees and fell, striking random stones, glancing off, then pattering to a stop in the pine needles. He hadn't aimed at anything at all, and he didn't look at me.

"He told her last night that he's not staying here, that he doesn't want to farm," Grover whispered.

I tried to imagine why Grover's father would tell his wife these things. To make her worry? What kind of cruelty would it take to say such a thing to a woman so sick and weak?

Grover glanced at me, then away again. "Katie,

I hate him. I won't stay with him. But what'll I do?"

"You'll make your own way," I said. "Mrs. Kyler says some of us just have to."

He knelt and kissed the stones that covered his mother and then stood up and began to walk. I trotted the Mustang to catch up and we fell in beside Grover. All that day we walked behind the wagons, neither one of us saying anything more. I just stayed close. There was nothing else I could do.

CHAPTER TEN

❧ ❧ ❧

The little one is weary now. She walks more slowly. We must settle for winter soon. It is time to find a valley with water and grass. It is time to stop traveling.

"Today ought to get us to The Dalles," Mr. McMahon said one morning, reading from his handbook. Then he lifted his head and shouted it out. I heard Charles Kyler holler the news to Mr. Taylor and, in seconds, everyone knew. A ragged little cheer went up from the wagons. I heard Miss Liddy's voice, high, happy, and *loud*. The Mustang shook his head and danced a little, then settled back into the long-strided walk that I had learned to keep pace with.

I had gotten into the habit of traveling not too far

from Mr. Heldon's wagon. Grover would sometimes come walk with me and the Mustang. That morning I heard Mr. Heldon's angry voice, and I angled closer.

"I don't care what you say," Mr. Heldon was saying. "If you'd taken better care of her..." He dropped his voice, and I couldn't hear the rest, but I could imagine it.

I caught my breath. It was the cruelest thing I could imagine anyone saying. And it wasn't true. No one could have done more to help someone than Grover had done for his mother. I slowed and started looking for grass for the Mustang before Mr. Heldon noticed me.

After a little while, Grover saw me and dropped back to walk with me for an hour or two. Then he drifted toward Andrew and the stock. I saw him helping herd the animals.

At noon, I went and got Grover, and he ate at Mrs. Kyler's campfire with me. He helped us clean up and then walked alongside the Kylers' wagon the rest of the day. His father didn't seem to know or care where he had gone.

We got to The Dalles before sundown. The town had been built near a narrow chasm that the mighty

Columbia River roared through. We could hear it from our camp—which was nearly a mile from town. We stayed back that far to find grass for the stock; closer to town, it was all grazed flat.

Most of us walked on once camp was made, just to see if the guidebooks were true. They were. There was a place where the wagon ruts simply stopped. Wagons could go no farther because of the river. We all stood staring at it.

The Columbia River was wide and deep, the color of a storm sky, and it muscled its way past, the currents swirling and twined. You couldn't hear anyone unless they shouted.

The sheer size and force of the river scared me. I could tell it scared everyone. We saw two Indian men walk past, carrying three canoes lashed together on their backs. Was that how people got across? No one said much walking back to camp.

We weren't the only ones there, and the next day we talked to other people. My fears were true. They were all waiting, camped out in a mile-wide circle outside the town, for Indian men who hired out their canoes as ferries to take them downriver and land them on the far side. We were told it could be a week or more, that it was first come, first across.

The next morning I left the Mustang with Andrew Kyler's herd, and Grover and I walked down to watch. The roaring of the wide river was enough to caution anyone about getting into a real, flat-bottomed, wide-decked ferryboat—never mind the swaying, makeshift canoe ferries.

Three and four canoes had been lashed together with planks fixed on top to make a platform. People were removing their wagon wheels so the wagon beds would lay flat on the platforms.

"Look," Grover said, pointing. I turned. As we stood watching, one of the ferries—a trio of canoes lashed together with a wheeless wagon perched on top—started downriver. The Indian men seemed incredibly skilled at maneuvering it, but when it went over a swirling set of rapids, it broke apart. The wagon tipped and we heard people screaming as they were thrown into the rushing water. No one drowned, thanks to the strength and wit of the Indian men, but the wagon was lost; seeing the accident made all of us even more uneasy.

On the way back, I told Mrs. Kyler I wanted to go into town to ask about my uncle. She nodded and asked if I wanted company. I told her no, that I was fine, even though it wasn't all that true. Every time I asked after my uncle, my hopes rose—and it hurt something awful when they fell again.

I was a long ways down the path toward town when I heard someone running behind me. Grover caught up, breathing hard. "Mrs. Kyler says I am supposed to keep an eye on you," he said between breaths.

"I don't really need anyone to come along," I told him.

"But do you mind if I do?" he interrupted. "Mrs. Kyler will be upset if I don't."

I sighed and shook my head. "I don't mind, Grover, I'm just scared." He nodded and I knew he understood.

"If I see my father, I am going to hide from him," he said quietly. "He'll be drinking by now."

I nodded and felt terrible for forgetting that my troubles were no bigger than anyone else's.

Grover gathered up his shirttails as we walked, shoving them down into his trouser waist. For an instant, I saw him as a stranger might. His hair was long and scraggly, his shirt had been patched, and a long tear crossed the left knee of his trousers. I looked down at my stained dress and thought about the picture we must make. Then, as we got closer to town, I realized that most of the people on the streets looked just like we did—weary, dirty, and ragged.

I glanced at Grover. "We'll just try in the shops."

He nodded and followed me, barely saying a word as we went from one end of the main street to the other, then crossed the street and started back up the other side. It was discouraging. Nary a soul had ever heard of Jack Rose. I started walking faster, my head down. I was trying not to cry. Grover just lengthened his step and tried to keep up as I hurried into—then out of—a half-dozen shop doors. No one knew anything about my uncle.

"It doesn't mean anything, Katie," Grover said as we neared the end of the street. "People just come through here—thousands of them. The shopkeepers don't get to know hardly any of them."

I took a deep breath. "I hope you're right."

He took a skip-step to come up beside me. "You know I am. It'll be someone in Oregon City who knows where he lives. Not here."

I nodded. "I just get scared."

"Let's try there before you give up," Grover said

as we neared the end of the street where we had started. He was pointing at a dry goods store. I slowed. He was right. No matter how upset I was, it was silly not to keep asking.

The shopkeeper was rearranging dusty bolts of cloth when we came in. He had never heard of Jack Rose. But he was talkative. He asked me a lot of questions about where we were from, how long it had taken to get across, how much farther we intended to go.

"All the way to Oregon City," I told him. "But I'm scared of the river," I admitted.

He grinned. "I wouldn't take one of them canoe ferries if there was gold on the other side. D'yer folks know about the Barlow Road?"

Grover and I shook our heads. Neither one of us had ever heard of it.

"There's a toll, and it's steep, but it keeps you off the river in those dang canoes."

"We'll tell the men in our party," Grover said, and thanked him.

I stepped back onto the boardwalk feeling a little lighter. It was finished. No one in The Dalles knew my uncle, and I could stop worrying about it.

Someone in Oregon City would. And I was glad to learn about the Barlow Road. Staying off the river made perfect sense to me, and I was pretty sure Mr. Kyler and the other menfolk would feel the same way.

They did. There wasn't even an argument about it. Everyone had seen or heard about the canoe ferry breaking apart. So we took the Barlow Road the next morning. We had to pay five dollars per wagon, and Andrew paid by the head for his herd. It was expensive, especially now when most people had spent too much of their savings already and wanted to put every penny toward tools and seed for their new farms. Still, no one balked.

The man in The Dalles had been right. It was a hard and terrible passage. The road was narrow and steep, barely a road at all. It was full of fist-sized stones that stubbed our toes and made the oxen and horses footsore.

We weren't the only ones on the toll road, though. A lot of people had decided climbing a mountain on a brand-new road was better than facing that river. We couldn't travel fast, but the people behind us never caught up or wanted to pass us. Everyone was weary. It was hard enough to keep moving.

Grover walked with me most days. He barely said a word. He was hungry all the time and would take food from Mrs. Kyler only when he couldn't stand it anymore. His father had no supplies, He had used the last of their money to buy whiskey in The Dalles. He swayed and slumped on the wagon bench and growled at anyone who tried to talk to him.

Mr. Kyler and Mr. Craggett had paid his wagon toll, and I was sure they had done it for Grover. The other men tolerated Mr. Heldon and his drinking only because they felt sorry for him, losing his wife, and because they knew there was so little distance left to travel before they could be shut of him forever. He had told everyone he intended to travel on as soon as he could.

Grover avoided his father entirely if he could, and the awful thing was that his father didn't even come looking for him when he slept night after night by the Kylers' campfire in blankets Mrs. Kyler loaned him.

Grover practiced juggling stones almost every moment he was awake—standing, walking, or sitting down. He was getting good at it. I saw him talking to Mr. Swann a few times, and it looked like he was learning different patterns. I was glad. He wanted to go with them, and I hoped they would let him.

Sometimes I dropped back and led the Mustang alongside Andrew Kyler and the stock. I liked being around Delia and Midnight, and sometimes I put halters on them and took all three horses looking for grass.

Delia was calmer than I remembered her being, and Midnight had somehow become really affectionate. She rubbed her forehead on my shoulder and nibbled at my fingers when I patted her. The rest of the horses seemed worn out and cranky. Delia and Midnight seemed content. I began to think that they had missed my company. I was sure they liked being around the Mustang, too, so I took them grazing as often as I could.

I found myself talking aloud to the Mustang more and more when I was off with the three horses by myself. I told him how scared I was and he stood close to me and blew his warm, windy breath across my face and down the collar of my dress. I was so glad to have him as my friend, so grateful he was with me. I told him that, too. He tossed his head and whinnied, long and loud, as though he had understood me. It echoed off the mountainside.

CHAPTER ELEVEN

☙ ☙ ☙

The earth softened beneath my hooves as we went.
The grass in the valley was good. The pine forests in the
mountains were green and thick.

s we came down into the Willamette Valley,
everyone began to brighten a little. It was
beautiful land. This was the place the Kylers had
dreamed of farming. This was the land the Taylors
and the Craggetts had wanted more than anything.
The McMahons were smiling, even Toby.

Mr. Kyler dragged his saddle out of the wagon
and began riding off to look for land. So did the
other men. They'd ride back near sundown and tell
the others what they had seen. It all sounded good.
I began to get excited again. If the farmland was all

good and so much of it still unclaimed, then there was a good chance that my uncle Jack was doing well, that he would be able to take me in. I kept an eye on Grover. He spent most days with Andrew Kyler now, helping with the stock. I knew he wanted to earn his suppers.

Mr. McMahon and Mr. Taylor hoped to be neighbors, and they began to ride the valley together as we traveled, too, looking for 640-acre plots that bordered on each other.

Mr. Silas and his friends packed up one morning and left. No one had any idea where they were going or why. We all stared after them. They headed southwest—that's all we would ever know.

The Craggetts had been quiet and grim for months, and they were thawing out now, chatting more with everyone and looking for land. Mrs. Craggett still walked out of her way to avoid talking to Miss Liddy.

I remembered the times that Miss Liddy had done more than her share for everyone's safety. I made myself a promise that I would never treat anyone like Mrs. Craggett treated Miss Liddy.

Miss Liddy and her friends weren't looking for

land—and they spent the time practicing their show. I got to ride Genevieve a little, and one evening I managed to stand on her back for a stride or two before I had to slide down and sit astride again. It was thrilling.

Oregon City was a bustling place the day we got there. The Willamette River was wide and deep, and the mill wheels for a sawmill and a gristmill turned steadily as we passed them. There were shops and stores up and down the long street we came in on. No one so much as looked up when we went by— until Miss Liddy's party drew close.

Genevieve, with Miss Liddy riding tall—and without bridle or saddle—led the way. The other horses were tethered behind the wagons, and people stared at their odd coloring and conformation. Mr. Swann, Mr. Dillard, and Mr. La Croix had changed into bright-colored shirts, and Miss Liddy wore a hat with an ostrich plume.

Grover and I watched the faces of the people on the sidewalks change as they spotted Miss Liddy. Some people actually gaped. We didn't laugh aloud, but we kept having to bite our lips.

The wagons had been draped with red and yellow

banners that read MᴄKᴇɴɴᴀ Cɪʀᴄᴜs Co. I was sure they would give a show as soon as they could. If they waited too long, winter weather would set in. At least we would get to see that before they left.

We went through town, then kept going. We passed four or five other wagon camps and finally camped along a slough a couple of miles north of town at the base of a swale that led back up into the mountains. No one knew how long it would take them to find land to claim, and the stock would need water and grass.

The nights were getting chilly, and Mrs. Kyler insisted that Grover and I both borrow more blankets from her. The next morning, I wanted to go into town and begin asking about my family. I waited until after morning chores and went to make sure the Mustang was settled with the herd before I told Mrs. Kyler.

"It's about a half hour's walk or a little more each way," she said. "You make sure you get back before dark." She looked past me. "Grover? Will you go with her?"

He nodded.

She smiled at me. "Good luck, Katie."

As we walked toward town, I glanced at Grover. "I will have to tell my uncle about the fever, about my parents and sister."

Grover exhaled slowly. "That will be hard news to bring him, Katie."

We walked for a time without saying anything else. I thought about how I would say it, how I would explain. I would have to tell him about the Stevenses and Hiram, too.

Grover picked a grass stem and chewed at the sweet end, then sighed and turned to me. "He will be glad to see you. I wish I had an uncle." He was silent another long moment, then he said, "I'm going to run away, Katie. I have to get clear of my father one way or another."

I met his eyes. "Maybe my uncle Jack can take you in, too."

Grover looked at me, blinking, his face lighting up. "I'd like that, Katie. I'd work hard for my keep."

I nodded. "I know you would."

Grover smiled. I lifted my chin as we got to the outskirts of town. I would go into every place in town, then stop farmers on the road if I had to. My uncle Jack was here somewhere, and I intended to find him.

The street was full of people, and we had to thread our way through the crowds. The first place was a hotel. The owner there said he had never heard of my uncle. Neither had the desk clerk nor a woman who was cleaning the floor with lye soap.

The livery stable was next to the hotel. It was big and full of spent-looking horses. "Never heard the name," the man said. "But I don't go to the saloons, and I don't talk to all that many folks. Your party have stock to sell?"

"We'll let our folks know that you buy," Grover said. The man turned back to his work.

"Your uncle could be farming somewhere a ways out of Oregon City," Grover said as we went on. "Maybe he doesn't come to town much."

I nodded and smiled at him, determined not to scare myself any more. We walked into three more establishments, and no one had heard of my uncle in any of them. Then we talked to two men who were working at the blacksmith's forge.

One of them scratched his head. "Never heard of him." He rubbed his eyes. "No, wait."

My heart leapt. I glanced at Grover, and he smiled at me. I held my breath.

"That's the man got in trouble over a card game, ain't it, Pete? The one who owed Sam Preston all that money?"

The man pumping the forge bellows paused in his work. "Maybe so. Yes, I believe it was. Jack Rose. Head of black hair, blue eyes—tall fellow. I heard he went to California by wagon. I also heard he jumped a ship in San Francisco and went whaling. Either way, he hasn't been in Oregon country in more than two years, miss."

I felt Grover take my hand. I don't remember thanking the men or even walking back into the rutted dirt street. All I remember is that Grover walked me along until I was steady on my feet again. Then he let go of my hand and moved off, but not too far.

"I should have known," I said as we got closer to the wagons. "I just *wanted* him to be here so bad." I wiped at my eyes and drew a shuddering breath. I started to cry. "I wanted him to have a nice wife and two daughters about my age."

I shook my head at how silly it all sounded, even to me. I had been believing a daydream. And now, here I was, two thousand miles from Iowa and no closer to having a home than I had been when I lived with the Stevenses.

"You all right?" Mrs. Kyler called when she saw us coming. I knew my face was blotchy from crying.

"Katie? Did you find out something?"

I nodded and bit at my lower lip. "He isn't here. He got into some kind of trouble and went off to California two years ago."

"Ah, child," Mrs. Kyler said. "Oh, Katie, I am so sorry." Before she could say or do anything else, I ran off, picking up my dress hem so I could go faster. I heard Grover call me, but I didn't answer. I just kept running until I had the Mustang on his lead, then I ran again, with him trotting beside me.

I didn't stop until the Mustang and I were a mile above the camp. The wagons looked like toys in the distance, and I was breathing hard.

I told the Mustang everything. He grazed quietly, lifting his head now and then to nuzzle at my face and neck. There was a breeze rising, and it fluttered my skirt as I started off again.

The Mustang moved with me, as he always did. I kept on, walking stiff-kneed, my hands clenched. I was so angry with myself. I felt so stupid and so

helpless. What could I do now? The Kylers were wonderful people, kind and good. But they were getting old, and they had a big family of their own, all grown up and married, and they had grandchildren born—and unborn—to think about. The last thing they needed was an orphan girl begging for a place. And poor Grover. I had all but promised him. Maybe the Kylers would take him in. I hoped so.

They had never once talked about my staying with them and why would they? Farming the first few years would be rough. There would barely be enough to eat for the people or the stock.

Andrew had offered to buy the stallion; he had never offered me a place in his family. He had one baby, and his wife was pregnant. Taking someone in meant sharing scarce food. The Mustang blew a long, warm breath along the nape of my neck, and I looked at him.

"If Miss Liddy will have me, maybe we can ..." I trailed off. It would be a long time before I could ride well enough to add anything to their show. And maybe I would never get good enough. Miss Liddy was no one's fool. She hadn't offered me a

place in her company, and there was no reason on the green earth why she would.

My thoughts were such an unhappy tangle as I kept walking uphill that I was wading through good, tall grass without even noticing it until the Mustang tugged at the rope. I stopped and he fell to grazing.

I wanted to cry, but I couldn't. I was beyond crying, and I leaned against the Mustang's shoulder, moving when he did, letting my thoughts spin because I could not stop them. I could hear birds overhead and the sighing of the breeze and the sound of the Mustang tearing grass off in eager mouthfuls. It was as though everything else in the world had disappeared.

Then the Mustang lifted his head so sharply that I turned, expecting to see someone or something coming toward us. Grover? But no one was there.

The Mustang lowered his head again. He was half starved from the hard miles in the sagebrush country and the mountain pass we had come over. He hadn't seen grass like this in months. "Good," I told him. I took a deep breath. "Tomorrow morning, we can bring the mares up here and—"

The Mustang struck at the ground with one hind

hoof and tossed his head, arching his neck. I fell silent. He turned away from me and faced the wind. I moved closer to him. "What?" He blew out a long breath and lifted his head to scent the air.

I tugged gently at the lead rope, but he didn't react. "If it's a wolf or something, we should start back now." I looked over my shoulder toward the wagons, expecting to see the tiny white dots of the canvas covers in the distance. But the swale had curved, and I couldn't see them.

The Mustang pawed at the earth. I couldn't spot whatever it was he had scented. But it didn't matter; it was smarter to go back. I turned, expecting the Mustang to turn with me, but he didn't. I was so surprised that I stumbled, jerking on the lead rope without meaning to. The stallion was startled into rearing.

I instinctively loosened my grip on the rope to keep from being dragged upward as I scrambled aside and waited for him to settle. But he didn't. He pranced a little, then shook his mane and reared again.

"Easy now. Just be easy," I singsonged, scanning the woods upwind. I couldn't see anything, but that didn't mean much. "Come on. Let's go." I tugged gently at the rope, but he didn't respond at all. "I'll bring you back here in the morning," I promised him. He refused to move.

I was nervous. I couldn't remember his ever acting like this. I had no idea how long it would take to gentle him into following me back, but I knew I shouldn't have come this far out of sight without telling someone. Mrs. Kyler would worry. So would Grover, I was sure. I'd just been so upset that all I had wanted was to get away from everyone.

"Please," I begged the Mustang, talking to him the way I always had. I explained that people would worry about us, that it was time to go back now.

He tossed his head and nickered.

It was only then that I heard a rustling sound and what sounded like footsteps in the trees below us. I held my breath and lifted my head. "Grover? Is that you?"

The Mustang nickered again, and I pulled hard at the lead rope. He turned to look at me, then faced the wind and nickered once more. "Grover?" I called. It was then I heard an answer. It wasn't meant for me, though. It was a whinny.

Now that I knew what I was looking for, I spotted the mare. She was a honey-colored horse with a long dark mane and tail. She eased back into the trees just as I saw a deep sorrel pass farther down the hill. Peering through the branches, I could see three more mares, all sleek and fit.

The Mustang shook his head hard and pulled at the rope. I tried to turn him toward me again. He dragged me forward a little ways. The mare whinnied again. He answered her.

There was no squealing challenge this time. For whatever reason, these mares seemed to be without a stallion. I saw two more threading their way through the pines, a gray and a tall chestnut.

The stallion turned, and I saw an expression in his eyes that had nothing to do with me. It was as though someone had lit a lantern inside him. I felt my eyes fill with tears. I might never find my home, but he had. This Oregon country was where he had been caught. All he needed was for me to take the halter off and let him go.

I began to cry hard. Everything that mattered to me was gone, had been taken away, all at once. But I knew what was right. I loved the Mustang. He had been my friend when I had no other in all the world.

My hands were shaking, and my vision was blurred with tears, but I knew what I had to do. I would not pay him back for his good heart by keeping him from *his* home.

Choking back sobs, I unbuckled the halter and slid it off over his ears. He turned to nuzzle my cheek, then he shook his head and rubbed his muzzle on one extended foreleg, scratching, erasing the marks in his coat from the leather straps.

He took a few steps, and I caught my breath. Then he stopped and looked back at me. "Good-bye," I whispered to him. "Thank you." He looked at me for a long moment, his eyes deep and kind.

Then one of the mares whinnied. Involuntarily, I reached out as the Mustang whirled around, reared, then lunged into a canter down the slope. I lowered my arm slowly, my heart aching as I watched him disappear into the forest. The hoofbeats and nickering got louder, then faded slowly into silence.

For a long time I stood, motionless, listening, feeling empty and scared and alone. I coiled up the lead rope and slung the halter over my shoulder and started back toward the wagons. It was the longest walk of my life. I stopped twice to weep, and I couldn't help turning back, over and over, trying to spot him, to hear him, but he was gone.

By the time I got back to camp I was pretty much past crying. I knew I had done the right thing. I knew it. And it still hurt like fire and weighed like stone on my heart.

CHAPTER TWELVE

❧ ❧ ❧

The little one brought me home. All that long, terrible
way, she was leading me to sweet grass and pine
trees. I will lead the mares far away from the two-leggeds
and the oxen that graze the grass to the ground.
Winter is coming. I must find a sheltered valley with
good grass for them, a place where foals can be
born and grow strong come spring.

I woke up the next morning and remembered
that the Mustang wasn't there. A weight settled
onto my spirits that seemed too much to carry. My
daydream about living with my uncle Jack was gone—
and so was my best friend. I felt sad and numb. I
felt like I had left my own heart on that mountainside. Day after day, I plodded through my chores.
Mrs. Kyler was watching me and so was Grover,
but they left me alone, and I was grateful.

Life in the camp went on. Every family was looking
for land. I helped Mrs. Kyler as always and waited

for her to tell me I needed to make some arrangement in town, find some employment. I still walked the mares every morning, looking for grass. It helped me to be around them, as odd as that may sound, because I knew they missed the Mustang, too, in their way.

Most evenings, I helped Mrs. Kyler make supper, then walked out to visit with Midnight and Delia before I went to bed. I usually cried a little, and the mares seemed to understand. One evening, Andrew was going through the herd, checking the horses. He thanked me for taking special care of them.

"They eat every blade of grass I can find for them," I told him. "Delia's flanks are all filled in, and Midnight's almost are. They're both putting on weight faster than any of the others."

The instant the words left my lips, I heard what I had said and understood. I blushed. He grinned, and I knew I was right. I stared at him, delighted. "They're both in foal? How long have you known?"

He smiled again. "A month or two."

I was astounded. "Why didn't you tell me?"

He shrugged. "I probably should have. I didn't want you and my mother worrying about one more thing every time we had to come across rough country or ford a river."

I stood still, a weight easing off my heart. Two foals. The Mustang had sired *two* foals. Maybe one would look like him. Maybe both would. I grinned, picturing them playing, leaping and running on Andrew's farm, racing across his good grassland.

"It's such grand news," Andrew said. "I was hoping for one. I didn't ever think we'd get this lucky."

I met his eyes. "May I come to see them? I don't know where I will end up, but, please, can I just come see them sometimes?"

Andrew was studying my face, and he chuckled. "My mother made me promise that if we got two, I'd give you one once it was old enough. I know better than to cross my mother."

I stared at him as though he was speaking some language I had never heard before. He patted my shoulder. "Close your mouth, Katie. You'll catch a fly."

I whirled and ran back toward Mrs. Kyler's wagon. She grinned when she saw me coming, and I whooped like Miss Liddy did sometimes, high and loud.

"Figured it out, did you, finally?" she teased.

I stamped one foot, pretending to be upset. "Everyone knew?"

She nodded. "We're all so pleased about it."

"Why didn't anyone tell me?"

She reached out and patted my cheek. "I thought losing the Mustang was something you needed to get used to first," she said. "Was I wrong?"

I didn't know what to say, so I hugged her, hard. She smelled like wood smoke and soap, and, for a minute, I didn't think about anything except how kind she was, how much I loved her.

"I don't know where I will end up," I began, "but if I can't take care of the foal right off, will Andrew keep it for me until I can?"

She nodded solemnly. "I am sure he would."

I danced a little jig, hopping in a silly circle. She laughed. So did I. It felt both strange and wonderful at the same time. I noticed Julia and Polly watching me from a distance. They smiled and waved, and I knew they were glad for me.

The next evening, Miss Liddy came into the Kylers' camp. Grover and I were eating second helpings of Mrs. Kyler's beans when Miss Liddy pulled a cracker box close the fire to sit upon.

Mrs. Kyler sat across from her. "My husband and I have been talking. We have an offer to make you, Grover." Mr. Kyler was leaning against the wagon, and he nodded.

I glanced at Grover. He had stopped chewing and stared at Mrs. Kyler, his eyes full hope.

Mrs. Kyler leaned down and put a stick of deadwood across the fire. It flared up, sparks floating upward into the ink-dark sky.

"And you, too, Katie," she added. "Miss Liddy and I have already made our bargain."

I blinked and looked at Miss Liddy.

She smiled at me. "Mr. Kyler is about to settle his land claim. In exchange for our help building cabins for the winter, tending stock, whatever needs doing, they will let us all winter on their place. Me, Jacob, James, Pierre—and both of you."

Grover and I exchanged another quick glance. My heart was racketing inside my chest.

"Andrew says you work miracles with the horses, Katie," Mrs. Kyler said, "and everyone knows how hard both you and Grover can work."

"And come spring," Miss Liddy said, "we can all talk again and decide what's best for everyone."

She winked at Grover. "You can practice all winter." Then she looked at me. "And we'll work on your riding when the weather lets us."

I turned to stare at Mrs. Kyler. Her face was full of kindness. Tears were stinging at my eyes, but I blinked them back. This wasn't a time to cry. I was going to be all right. I hadn't found my own family, but I had ended up with friends so close they might as well be.

I exhaled slowly, taking it in. Hiram would be so pleased when I wrote him. So would Annie. They weren't really my family either, but...I glanced at Grover. Having family was no guarantee of having love.

"Yes?" Mrs. Kyler said, looking between us. "Do we have a bargain?"

Grover and I both nodded.

"And you can come back whenever you like," she said to Liddy. Then she looked at me and Grover. "If you leave, you can always come back."

I smiled, breathing in the cool, soft Oregon air. Grover shot me a look so full of joy and relief that I grinned at him.

I looked up at the sky and knew that the Mustang

was somewhere under the same stars, standing watch and guarding his herd. He had found his home. And maybe I had found mine. Maybe I had.